Picture Perfect

HART LAND ~ BOOK TEN

CHRIS KENISTON

Indie House Publishing

BOOKS BY CHRIS KENISTON

Hart Land
Heather
Lily
Violet
Iris
Hyacinth
Rose
Calytrix
Zinnia
Poppy
Picture Perfect

Farraday Country
Adam
Brooks
Connor
Declan
Ethan
Finn
Grace
Hannah
Ian
Jamison
Keeping Eileen
Loving Chloe
Morgan
Neil

Aloha Series Heartwarming Edition:
Aloha Texas
Almost Paradise
Mai Tai Marriage
Dive Into You
Look of Love
Love by Design
Love Walks In
Shell Game
Flirting with Paradise

Surf's Up Flirts:
(Aloha Series Companions)
Shall We Dance
Love on Tap
Head Over Heels
Perfect Match
Just One Kiss
It Had to Be You
Cat's Meow

Honeymoon Series
Honeymoon for One
Honeymoon for Three
Honeymoon for Four

ACKNOWLEDGMENT

This has been an interesting year for my family. My mother's Alzheimer's is progressing and we've had to make lots of changes. Through it all I have dear friends and family who keep things moving along. Without everyone's support I doubt I'd ever find time to write another word.

Thanks go out to my daughter who loves me even when I get grumpy, my cousin-in-law Shilo who has been a massive blessing to my team, and especially my dear friend Olivia Sands for her moral support and hand in my plotting help.

Escaping for a short while with the Hart clan has been a wonderful time for me and I hope you enjoy visiting with them as much as I have!

CHAPTER ONE

"I need a nice girl like I need a hole in my head." Glenn Peterson had been down that road. He'd learned the hard way that he had lousy judgment. Tall, pretty and polite, his ex Amanda came from a large family she adored. Somehow he'd confused her sweet smile and attention with a strong foundation for a loving future.

"What does visiting your brother have to do with a nice girl?" His grandfather might not have said outright that Glenn needed to get over his poor judgment and find another wife, but he knew it was coming.

He and his grandparents had been doing this dance since the day his divorce was final. "I still remember whose idea it was for Alan to hibernate at Hart Land." Of course meeting Cindy had been the best thing that ever happened to his brother, but that didn't change the fact that Glenn did not need a wife.

"You do remember that Harold is out of granddaughters'?"

"A technicality." Decades of military training and experience made these two old men brilliant strategists. Glenn wasn't taking any chances. Though deep down he really did want to spend the holidays with his brother and his wife.

"You are too suspicious." He could almost see

his grandfather shaking his head. "Your grandmother and I will be arriving on Christmas Eve. It would be wonderful to have all of us together again for the holidays."

Glenn stabbed at the dried out leftover chicken. Separated for over a decade, his grandparents had once again rekindled their relationship. Apparently his grandfather had learned a hard lesson or two in his old age. Visions of his grandmother laughing, his grandfather pretending to love her eggnog, and sitting around the table with his brother enjoying mountains of home cooked treats had Glenn reconsidering his decision to spend the holidays skiing with strangers. Even if he expected at least some of those strangers to be of the decidedly female persuasion. After all, he'd never sworn off women all together, just the ones with wedding bells on their minds. And of course, the overly ambitious.

"Oops. Your grandmother is calling me. Have to run. At least think about joining us. I promise, no matchmaking shenanigans."

"Give Grams my love."

"Will do."

The call disconnected and Glenn debated eating the now cold dry chicken, or placing it back in the microwave and eating warm dry leftover chicken. The phone rang, flashing his brother's number. Gramps didn't waste any time. "Hello."

"How's life in sunny California?" Alan always asked the same thing.

"Dry." And Glenn usually answered the same. The old song "It Never Rains in California" popped into his head. They'd grown up in a military family, chasing the world. He'd briefly considered a military career and after a few years with Uncle Sam, quickly changed his mind. Now there was no moving him from his comfortable—and sunny—abode. "So, what did Gramps have to say?"

"About what?" Alan's tone dropped.

Maybe Glenn had overreacted. Perhaps his grandfather hadn't hung up and called Alan to gang up on him. "Christmas."

A sigh of relief sounded through the line. "Okay, that's not so bad. Gramps and Grams are at an age where answering the phone might hold a litany of bad news. One of those calls is right up there with letting me know you accepted an exceptional offer someplace impossible to reach easily, like Antarctica."

"No one really lives in Antarctica." He was pretty sure the only permanent living things near the South Pole were penguins.

"Doesn't matter. Though I wouldn't object if you took a job that kept you on the East Coast."

Now his brother sounded like his ex wife. "Sorry, I like it just fine here." Most of the time.

"I know, I know. So what were you saying about Christmas?"

"I was on the phone with Gramps. He tried to talk me into joining you guys for the holidays."

"Not a bad idea. We haven't seen you since the wedding."

Every summer Glenn had good intentions to visit his brother, and every year life got in the way of his well intended plans. Having given up on the chicken, he threw the unappealing meal into the trash and stared out the kitchen window. Most people would kill for the sunny views with blue skies and palm trees. Very relaxing. Except, not terribly conducive to the Christmas spirit. A sudden longing for lights flickering on the tree, mistletoe hanging in doorways, and stockings hung by the fire-lit chimney with care surged from deep in his gut. "Is Cindy's sister still baking all those delicious morsels?"

"Lily? You bet. Her bakery has developed quite the reputation."

"What were those cookies she made for the rehearsal dinner?"

Alan laughed. "Spitzbubens. Those things are famous all across this mountain."

His cravings for all things White Christmas, including tasty desserts, escalated. "If the invitation is still on the table, I'd like to spend my Christmas break in Hart Land."

"Annie Leibovitz eat your heart out." Kelly Chambers scrolled through the images from her recent photoshoot and smiled. The red scarf draped at the steps of the otherwise all black and white photo of St Patrick's was brilliant. And it hadn't even been her idea. One of the crew had dropped it hurrying across the set and Kelly opted to keep it in. She'd been looking for just the right twist for the shoot at some of the more famous New York City landmarks, and a pop of a different color in every black and white picture had been the answer.

"There's trouble in paradise." Her assistant popped her head into Kelly's office and sighed. "Her Highness wants you in her office yesterday."

"Great." Hands on the desk, Kelly pushed to her feet. "Just once I'd like for her to rush me to her office to invite me out for dinner or a drink. Whatever she needs, it's going to be a pain in my butt *and* my ulcer. I just know it."

"You still going to spend the holidays in Florida with your cousin?"

"That's the plan. Unless Her Highness sends me to Timbuktu instead."

Her assistant followed her out the door and down the hall. "I'll keep my fingers crossed for you."

"May want to cross your toes too."

At her boss's door, Kelly sucked in a deep breath, closed her eyes, and slowly exhaled. Every instinctive nerve she had was loudly screaming this would be another one of those *you're a good egg* assignments that would find her at the last minute covering for someone else's screw up. One minute she was an award winning and coveted photographer at a fashion show in Milan and the next minute she'd be practically living in a freezer photographing a national butter carving contest. In the end, the sculptures were amazing but that assignment had been a sub zero nightmare for warm-weather-loving her to photograph. "You wanted to see me?"

"Yes." Her Highness, also known as Caroline, waved her in. "We have a situation."

Even though she knew this was coming, Kelly still braced herself.

"Elizabeth Myers has had another battle with her significant other and she can't *possibly*," Caroline paused to over enunciate the word as she waved her hand up in the air, "turn in the extravagant and soul sucking holiday story she'd planned in time to go to print."

"I see." Not that Kelly did see. She was a photographer, not a byline writer, but Elizabeth Myers had a reputation for being a bit of a drama queen and relatively unpredictable. Issues with her stories were also the magazines' bestsellers, so everyone put up with the woman's mood swings and temper tantrums.

"You're the only person I can count on who doesn't have a big family waiting for them at home with hearth and fire and Christmas tree."

And there it was again. A last minute assignment that would save Caroline's job and send Kelly who knew where. But, as much as she'd like to dig her indignant heels into Caroline's one inch thick carpet, her boss was right. Kelly's career had kept her moving and traveling around the world with no time to work on home or hearth. At least with a husband and two kids, her cousin would be ready with a Christmas tree.

"We're going to go with a straight holiday photo shoot. No time for a byline, but if the pictures turn out the way I suspect, we can do a follow up for the next edition with New Year."

Kelly could feel that Christmas tree in Florida slipping away.

"Our esteemed CEO is friends with a retired General in New England. He has an inn with some solid reputation. The town is a bloody postcard for a Rockwellian winter. They spend weeks building up to Christmas Day. The perfect recipe for the kind of shoot the CEO wants. There should be plenty of opportunity to get some eye popping photos in time to hit the streets by Christmas Eve."

For a split second her jaw dropped and her mouth moved to form words of protest. Instead her brain engaged and she realized any argument would be futile. At least if she wanted to remain gainfully employed. There were way too many hungry young photographers nipping at her heels, dying to steal her job out from under her. "Where am I going?"

"Hart Land." Caroline handed her an envelope. "You'll be staying at the Inn. Everything you need is in the file, including the schedule of events. The holiday pageant is a big deal so make sure you get plenty of photos of the donkey."

"Donkey?" What was she getting into?

Without looking up, Caroline nodded. "The

nativity scene in front of the church has real people and a few animals. The donkey is apparently pretty popular. Probably stinks to high heaven, but they're pretty well known on Lawson Mountain. Will make great copy. Like I said, perfect recipe for a popular holiday edition. There may even be a cover shot in there somehow."

Caroline's phone rang and with a slight flick of the wrist, Kelly was dismissed. And on her way to small town USA… and donkeys.

CHAPTER TWO

Glenn hadn't realized how much snow would greet him in Lawford. Sure, his mind knew this was early December on a New England mountain and snow would be a fact of life, but he still didn't quite make the connection until he stepped out of the car and his leather loafers sank into six inches of white powder.

Opening the back door, he reached for the leash and tugged. Wooster was none too pleased at the prospect of diving into the snow. The animal was clearly smarter than he was.

"Come on, fella. I'm not going to carry you around for the entire visit. It's just snow. Cold water. You love water."

"Oh, how wonderful to see you again!" Arms open wide, oblivious to the chilled air, a tall woman in cream colored wool pants with matching long sleeve sweater and a bright blue knit shawl that reached her knees and accentuated her silver shoulder length hair, practically sailed down the front steps and enveloped him into the fold of her arms.

Apparently Wooster's love of a pretty woman outweighed his fear of cold paws. The tail wagging pup hopped out of the car and awkwardly loped over to Alan's grandmother-in-law.

"Well now, who are you?" As graciously as she'd greeted Glenn, Fiona Hart leaned over to scratch Wooster behind the ears and whisper something only the dog could hear.

"This is Wooster. Alan said bringing him would be okay. I hate to leave him in a kennel if I don't have to."

"Of course it's fine. My husband and I have two lovely Goldens. I'm sure they'll make friends. In the meantime, Alan will be here any minute. He and Cindy were held up by a stubborn bull moose that seemed to think no one else needed to use the road."

"Welcome! Welcome!" sounded from the top of the porch.

More names and faces were coming back to him. For the few days he'd been in town for Alan and Cindy's wedding, Glenn had been inundated with family and friends alike. But Fiona Hart and the family housekeeper Lucy were too memorable to forget. Mrs. Hart had an elegance and style that would have kept her on the cover of any high fashion magazine. As for Lucy, the family housekeeper could cook her way into any man's heart and permanent memory.

Brushing her hands together briskly, from her perch on the front porch, Lucy frantically waved him inside. "Hurry up now. Leave your luggage in the car. I'll send George out for it. No need to keep this door open heating the outdoors."

Fiona Hart slipped her hand into the crook of Glenn's arm. "Now Lucy, let's not rush our guest. A little winter chill does a body good."

"Maybe your body," Lucy muttered, still holding the door for them. As he passed over the threshold, Lucy glanced at his feet. "You did bring boots, didn't you?"

As much as he hated to, Glenn shook his head. There wasn't much of a need for winter boots in Southern California. Though he'd meant to pick up a pair if he'd gone skiing in Tahoe, he'd just run out of time.

"Well, don't you worry about it. We have plenty of spares." Fiona somehow managed to smile at him and scowl at Lucy at the same time.

Meanwhile, Wooster must have gotten a whiff of whatever aroma was drifting over from the kitchen. His tail was now wagging at the speed of a crazed metronome and he was successfully dancing circles around everyone's feet.

Lucy lifted her chin and smiled proudly. "Dog knows a good pot roast when he smells it. My grandmother's secret recipe."

"He's going to have to do without." Glenn shrugged apologetically. "No people food."

Lucy glanced down at the dog, back up at him, then barely rolled her eyes before leading the way into the kitchen. Somehow, he had a feeling Wooster was about to have his first pot roast dinner tonight.

"Don't you mind her." Fiona patted Glenn's arm. "She just likes to spoil animals and people alike."

Once in the kitchen, Glenn's stomach growled and he realized he'd skipped breakfast and landed in a post lunch time zone.

Even though he was positive Lucy couldn't have heard his stomach from clear across the kitchen, by the time he'd crossed into the large room with a massive island, the housekeeper was doling out a bowl of chowder and slicing still warm bread. "We saved you lunch."

The temptation to kiss her on both cheeks like the French was overwhelming. Instead he settled for a broad smile and sincere thank you. He took a few slow sips, practically rolled his eyes back in his head, and swallowed a moan of pure pleasure. "This is the absolute best clam chowder I have ever had in my life."

Lucy beamed like the Cheshire Cat, but didn't say a word.

A few more spoonfuls and Glenn was actually tempted to give his dog a taste. *Dog*. Looking left and then right, Wooster was nowhere to be found in the kitchen.

"He wandered down the hall a few minutes ago. Probably sniffing out the territory." Fiona Hart seemed to read his mind. "He's house broken, correct?"

"He is."

"Then no reason to worry."

He wondered if this is how parents felt when teachers and other professionals told them not to worry about their children. Glenn wasn't feeling concern so much as... responsibility. There were a lot of nice things in the large Victorian entryway and throughout the first floor. Still, how much harm could a medium-sized loveable mutt get into in only a few minutes?

"Hey!" a loud shrill came from the other room two seconds before Wooster came scrambling into the kitchen, a flash of red in his mouth visible as the pup ran right past him and out the back doggie door.

"Uh oh," Lucy muttered.

The sound of a clack then thump repeatedly followed after each other. Glenn had gotten to his feet, poised to chase after Wooster and whatever damage he'd done, when hobbling on one bare foot and tugging at a shoe on the other, a dark haired beauty with fiery green eyes leaned against the door frame. "Which way did the thief go?"

"Thief?" Glenn didn't have time to ponder who the woman was referring to, both Fiona and Lucy were pointing at the back door.

Another look at the woman now stomping barefoot across the kitchen, one bright red shoe in her hand, and he knew Lucy was absolutely right. "Uh oh."

This was not a good sign for the start of this project. By the time Kelly had crossed the state line out of New York, the winter scenery had begun to lull her into a tranquil state of calm. By the time she'd crossed two more states, she'd begun to think that maybe this assignment to Santa Land on earth wasn't such a bad turn of events after all.

When the massive Victorian house decked out in colorful holiday lights peeked through the bare trees and pristine blanket of snow, she'd been taken back to a time and place she hadn't thought about for years. All the way back to when Christmas meant visiting her grandparents, baking cookies, and building snowmen. Oh yeah, and pretty packaged gifts that were just as much fun to open as to play with.

Even the high ceiling entryway that greeted her with a ten foot tree decked out in old fashioned garland, tinsel, and antique glass balls reminded her of why to a child Christmas and magic were almost synonymous. At the check in desk, leaning against the massive wooden piece of furniture, the hours behind the wheel and morning run-around in an effort to arrive at a decent time of day hit her. Lightly slipping out of one of her prized possessions, a pair of Jimmy Choo shoes she'd been gifted after a fashion shoot, an uncommon occurrence for a photographer, she stretched the aching toes on her left foot and was about to shift and stretch her other foot when a large mound of brown fur snatched the shoe and took off sliding across the gleaming wooden floor.

Just like when her parents divorced and turned Christmas into a game of tug of war, shattering all that was good and magical about the winter holiday, that mutt had just reminded her what the big bad world was all about. Glowing all nostalgic about Christmas was a fool's errand. One shoe on and one foot bare, she ran after the dog, screaming, "Thief!"

Turning at the doorway she'd spied the animal disappearing through, she came to a screeching halt at the sight of not one but three people staring wide-eyed at her. Tugging her remaining shoe off, she prepared to dash full speed after the mutt when her gaze fell on a rather impressive male specimen. Any other time and she would have searched for a wedding ring and maybe taken a few minutes to indulge in the illusion that there was still a nice single guy left in the world, but right now, she wanted her shoe. "Which way did the thief go?"

The two women—one she might want to talk to later about a private fashion shoot, the other wrapped in a large holiday themed apron that threatened to drag her back into the magical world of her grandmother's butter cookies with sprinkles—both pointed to the back door.

Dignity and urgency battling inside her, she opted to move quickly rather than dash across the floor like a crazed Cruella Deville. No sooner had she flung the door open than she spotted the culprit curled up at the opposite end of the narrow porch, chomping happily on her shoe.

"Uh oh," sounded from over her shoulder, two seconds before the tall man, who she now saw did not wear a wedding ring, inched around and snarled, "Wooster. Put that down."

More obedient than she would have imagined, the animal immediately dropped his jaw open, releasing the shoe, and somehow managed to look appropriately forlorn.

"You know better than that." The man stomped

heavily up to the dog, waving a very long, very slender finger at him. "You're too old to be snacking on shoes."

The man leaned over, picked up the shoe, and must have had at least a passing knowledge of high fashion footwear. The second his gaze saw the name etched across the sole of the shoe, she heard an almost painful wince cross his lips.

That was all she needed to hear to know she'd seen the last of her Jimmy Choos.

"I'm so very sorry. I will of course replace them." The man turned to face her, stretching out his arm, tooth marks covering her once favorite kitten heel pumps. "I really am so sorry."

She dared to retrieve the shoe, then slowly swallowed the disappointment. Living in an expensive place like New York City precluded anyone with her nice salary spending almost a thousand dollars on a pair of shoes. She was torn between wanting to scream or cry. "And they were comfortable too."

Not till he winced again did she see the pain and remorse in his gaze and realize she'd said that last thought out loud.

"Please let me make this up to you."

A gentle tap on her foot distracted her from the handsome man in front of her. All she needed now was for some forest animal, or worse vermin, to go scampering across her bare feet. The same brown mutt that had run off with her shoe sat at her feet looking more forlorn than its owner. Once the animal was sure it had her attention, he leaned back on his haunches, lifted both paws up in the air, and then waved one at her.

How the heck was anyone supposed to resist such cuteness? Even if it did just eat her favorite pair of shoes. Maybe when she got home she'd have to reconsider getting a dog. A small one. One who could travel in her purse on the airplane. And one who didn't eat shoes.

CHAPTER THREE

The Hart family dinner table had more people in the middle of the week than a White House gala. He couldn't begin to imagine what Christmas morning must have been like growing up in this tight knit family. For the most part Glenn was able to keep his sister-in-law's three siblings and their spouses organized, but he wasn't sure how good he would be at keeping up with every single one of the Hart grandchildren and their parents when they'd all be here for Christmas week.

Iris, the granddaughter from New York City who now lived on the mountain, had joined them for dinner alone. Her husband had returned yesterday from a business trip to an oil rig in the North Sea and claiming jet lag, had opted to skip the Hart family dinner tonight. Glenn had the feeling the choice for him to stay home with the kids was more an excuse to not overwhelm him with too many people. And right about now he was very thankful for it. "Are you all settled in?" she asked.

"I haven't even seen my cabin yet. Wooster created a little bit of havoc this afternoon just before Alan and Cindy arrived."

"Havoc?" Iris reached down to where Wooster rested at Glenn's feet and scratched behind the pooch's ear. "This sweet boy?"

"That sweet boy," Cindy shook her head at the dog, "ate a guest's Jimmy Choo shoe."

Iris' eyes opened wide. "You're kidding."

"I'm afraid not." Even Glenn recognized the designer name. Amanda, his ex-wife, had a closet full of shoes that cost more than the average person's monthly salary.

"How did she take it?"

"Actually," Fiona Hart smiled, "she took the mishap quite well."

"We met her on her way to her cabin." Cindy reached for her glass. "She seemed quite pleasant. Had that been me, I would have been a tad more on the grumpy side."

"Grumpy? You? Not possible." Alan grabbed his wife's hand and squeezed it. The heat in his gaze was so intense, it made Glenn feel like a voyeur.

Poppy reached for a second serving of blueberry pie and looked to her cousin Iris. "We don't get very many people wearing fancy shoes around here. Is she one of your old friends?"

Her grandmother looked to her New York granddaughter. "I don't think so. Her name is Kelly Chambers. She's here to do a magazine piece on small town Christmas."

"Nope. Not a friend of mine." Iris continued scratching at the puppy who now had rested his head on her lap. "Christmas is only weeks away. Wouldn't something for the holidays have been done and ready to publish months ago?"

"I was thinking the same thing." Callie, the sister who taught high school, eyed the pie as though debating how many laps it might take to work off another slice.

Cindy, seated at the right hand of her grandfather, scratched the back of a well-trained Golden Retriever. "I came in a little late on that conversation, but it sounded like whatever was planned for the holiday edition ran into some kind of snag and so this assignment is a last-minute fill-in."

"I wonder if she's last-minute because she's all they had available, or because she's really good?" Poppy stabbed at her pie.

"She's really good." Glenn reached for his water. Taking a sip, he noticed over the rim all eyes at the table were on him. He swallowed and shrugged. "I looked her up on the Internet. Most of her photo credits come from around the world and there's a list of awards longer than my arm. Her work is very well respected and yet, she also seems to do the occasional low profile shoots as well."

"Really?" Poppy's eyes danced with excitement. "I wonder if she could include a little bit about the bakery."

"Ooh." Callie looked up. "That could be fun."

"That's what I was thinking." Lucy came into the dining room carrying a fresh pot of coffee and refilled Glenn's mug. "Guest's first."

"Thank you." There were no words for how delicious everything that came out of the Hart kitchen tasted. The pot roast had been to die for. The sour cream blueberry pie was by far the best of any pie he had ever had in his life. She even managed to make an ordinary brew taste like an exotic blend. If he weren't so sour on marriage, he would gladly disregard the age difference and get down on bended knee right now.

Lucy strolled around the table, filling cups with fresh coffee. "I think having Kelly here is going to be a good thing for Lawford. A very good thing."

Glenn wasn't completely positive if Lucy had been specifically looking at him, or if perhaps he was just a tad paranoid after hearing about the Hart granddaughters, with a little nudge from the matchmaking family, had married one after another.

"Yes," Lucy repeated. "Very good."

Paranoid or not, Lucy definitely looked at him and smiled when she said very good. Maybe he should have gone skiing after all.

Despite the unpleasant turn of events today, the evening had been smooth sailing. For a brief while Kelly had regretted not accepting the Harts invitation to join them for dinner, but then one of the granddaughters had brought her a dinner tray with the best pot roast and garlic mashed potatoes she'd ever had. Living in New York City, Kelly had eaten at some of the best restaurants in the world, and she had never eaten a pot roast that melted in her mouth like butter.

Too stuffed to eat another bite, she'd sifted through the holiday season brochures on the coffee table. Her boss had already enlightened her on the lighting of the tree, which was why she'd arrived so early to catch the festivities tomorrow night on film. She'd also been aware of the live nativity scene, but a few things like the pageant and a popular nearby Santa's Village were news to her. Tired and mourning the loss of her favorite shoes, she'd opted to put work aside till tomorrow and instead curled up on the sofa with a new book. Occasionally, she glanced up at the roaring fire or out the window at the snow covered lake. Eventually the lone slice of pie on the kitchen counter that had teased her through five chapters won the battle of wills. No longer able to resist, she set the book aside and decided it was time to finish unpacking, slip into her jammies, and curl up in front of the fire again, this time with that delicious dessert, before calling it a night.

For a small family hotel, the Hart Land Inn paid amazing attention to detail. While she had been dealing with the shoe stealing dog, and then checking in, Lucy had arranged for her luggage to be placed in her cabin. The space was impeccable. The refrigerator was stocked, the bath towels were lush, and all she had needed to do to start the fire had been to strike a match. Though she wasn't really a breakfast person, she'd already decided that for the duration of her mountain stay, she could learn to indulge in fresh-baked breakfast foods.

Unzipping her suitcase, she emptied the bag and folded or hung her things in the drawers and closet. Normally she had no trouble living out of a suitcase, but if the magazine decided she needs to stay for more photos for another edition, she might as well make herself at home. And so far, the Harts were making that easy to do. Turning her attention to the dark corner of her bedroom where George the handyman had left her luggage, she grabbed a couple of camera bags from atop the pile and set them aside, surprised to discover the carry on with her makeup and other toiletries wasn't hers at all. "This makes no sense."

How did someone else's bag wind up in her room and where was her bag? The inner debate over whether or not to invade someone else's privacy to uncover the bag's owner ended abruptly when she decided she really needed her own bag back. As soon as she ate the pie that was still calling her name from the kitchenette, she would want to brush her teeth. Without a lock, the bag was easy to open. A small leather toiletry bag rested on top. Not a cheap bag, but nothing over the top expensive like her Jimmy Choo shoes. The initials GRP were emblazoned on the side, but that wasn't what told her who the bag belonged to. The gentle whiff of cologne set her nerves on edge the same way standing too close to Glenn Peterson had a few hours ago. How the heck had she wound up with his carry on? And did that mean he had hers? *Crud.* According to the clock on the nightstand, it wasn't all that late. She could take the bag up to the main house and maybe someone could call Glenn and retrieve her bag before bedtime. Or maybe they kept spare toothbrushes and toothpaste for guests who didn't pack everything they needed. Considering how well this place was stocked, she was a bit surprised there wasn't already an extra toothbrush in the bathroom.

Glenn's bag in hand, she nudged the front door shut and made her way up the path to the main house. Halfway up the walkway a shadowed figure came out of a cabin and turned in her direction. The tall, broad shouldered silhouette carrying a small bag had to be Glenn. And he had to be looking for her. Well, not her, his bag that she happened to have.

"Hi." He smiled softly as they drew closer. "I see you discovered the little mishap."

She nodded and held out the bag. Like a scene in an old movie, she reached for her bag, their fingers brushing ever so slightly against each other and like the scent of his cologne, the bare touch set her nerves on edge. What was it about this man that was so darn electric? "Here you go."

"Thanks." His bag in hand, he lifted hers a little higher. "I'm not sure how they got mixed up, but why don't you let me carry this back to your cabin."

"I was wondering the same thing when I spotted the unfamiliar bag. I guess maybe George isn't all that detail oriented." She smiled at him and waved at her bag. "It's not that heavy. I can take it."

"I don't mind, really. It's the least I can do."

"If you're still feeling guilty about the shoes,

please don't. Nothing is meant to last forever. Not even good shoes."

"That might be easier said than done."

She shook her head and waved her fingers in a hand-it-over gesture, almost afraid to touch again.

With a soft sigh of resignation, he handed her the bag. "Thank you again for returning my bag."

"My pleasure." Slowly, they each took a step back, then another before she turned around.

She'd made it a few steps when he called out, "Will I see you at breakfast?"

Looking over her shoulder, he was still walking backwards up the hill. If he wasn't careful he might trip over something. "That's the plan."

In the moonless night, she could make out the nod. "Good night."

It was hard to see if he was smiling or not, but she'd like to think so. She called out "good night" and once again turned toward her door. A ridiculous urge to skip the rest of the way washed over her. Maybe there really was just a little bit of magic in Hart Land.

CHAPTER FOUR

"Glad to see you join us." The broad smile Fiona Hart flashed at Kelly made her feel as though she were a member of the family.

"Waking up early came more easily than I'd thought."

"Trouble sleeping?" From his seat at the head of the table, with a Golden Retriever on either side, the General frowned.

Grabbing a dish from the end the buffet table, Kelly shook her head and smiled at the family patriarch. Tall, strong, and distinguished, he was everything one would expect from a retired Marine Corps officer. "Quite the contrary. From the moment my head hit the pillow, I slept like the proverbial log. It was quite nice."

"Mountain air has that affect on people." Porcelain cup in hand, Fiona took a sip of her morning tea.

Sleeping soundly through the night was something Kelly could easily get used to. She'd barely had time to take a seat at the table when she heard the patter of puppy nails against the hardwood floors. Glancing over at the dogs by the General's side, she could see neither one was moving. Both had heard the same sounds as she had, but noses to the air, they weren't leaving their master's side.

"Morning." Glenn Peterson came into the room,

Wooster at his heels. "Since the three dogs seemed to get along fine last night, I hoped as long as I keep a close eye on him, bringing Wooster wouldn't be a problem."

"Of course not." Fiona Hart gestured for him to take the seat beside Kelly.

With a brief nod, he went first to pour himself a cup of coffee then with a plate of scrambled eggs and bacon in hand, took his place at the table.

More conversation on how well did you sleep and mountain air made the rounds until the topic shifted to the first day of the Christmas festivities. Frankly, she was rather excited. "Does anyone in the family have a float in the parade?"

Fiona waved her hand back and forth in a gesture that implied sort of. "Not officially. We stopped entering ages ago when the grands were no longer little children. Last year and this year we do a little something for the next generation to participate but not an official entry."

"Wouldn't be fair anyhow." The General scratched behind both dog's ears. "Fiona and I have been on the judge's panel for over a decade."

"Some of the floats get wonderfully creative. My favorite is still the year the Bancroft family did the old lady who lived in the shoe, except the shoe was a Christmas stocking and all the kids were little elves. Very creative."

"Though I did think making the old woman Mrs. Claus was a tad too much."

Grinning at her breakfast guests, Fiona shook her head ever so slightly. "Don't you pay him no never mind. It was perfectly adorable."

Carrying a large platter with warm pancakes, Lucy walked over to the buffet. "Buttermilk pancakes. My grandmother's recipe. You'll want to eat them while they're hot."

"They're delightful cold too." Fiona dabbed at the corners of her mouth with her napkin. "But I do recommend trying them warm from the griddle."

A pot holder on either hand, Lucy spun about to face the table, her gaze settling on Glenn. "There will be plenty of deep discounts on the first day of the official Christmas countdown. I'd suggest you find your way to Main Street and get yourself a pair of warm and preferably waterproof boots."

He nodded. "That's the plan."

"And you." Lucy swiveled in place to face Kelly. "The shop decorations and parade will give you some of the best holiday photos. You won't want to miss any of it. Stores open an hour early today in preparation for the tree lighting tonight."

"Thank you," Kelly replied softly.

Already over the threshold, Lucy paused and looked over her shoulder. "Since Kelly has a car, you might want to ride together. No need to pack lunch, Mabel's will be serving her mac and cheese and tomato basil soup. Don't tell her I said this, but her soup is much better than mine."

"Nonsense." Fiona waved off her longtime housekeeper and cook, then leaned into the table conspiratorially. "Truth is, Mabel uses Lucy's recipe, but no one is supposed to know."

Wooster let out a woof and Kelly shifted her attention from her hostess, the quaint family secrets, and thoughts of how to possibly use the soup story in her layout, to the dog now nudging the Golden retriever twice his size out of his way. The big Golden opened one eye and then closed it. When Wooster woofed and nudged a second time, the dog actually sighed, rolled slightly to her side, and moved one paw, letting Wooster lay down beside her.

"Well, I'll be." Fiona grinned. "Looks like

Wooster and Lady have made friends."

The General bobbed his head. "If you two want to head into town, I'm sure Wooster will be fine here."

"Absolutely." Fiona clapped her hands together. "The town is very pet friendly, but after yesterday's little, uh, incident with the, um, shoe, shopping for boots with Wooster may not be advisable."

"Oh." Glenn set his fork down, glanced sheepishly at Kelly before turning his attention to their hostess. "You may have a point. Are you sure leaving him here will be all right? I don't want to put anyone out."

"I'm sure." Fiona smiled at him and took another sip of tea.

Glenn let out a short sigh and straightening in his seat, faced Kelly. "Would you mind if I hitched a ride with you into town?"

"Not at all." At this moment, she couldn't think of anyone else she'd rather explore with.

Glenn had never been so intrigued at the idea of wandering about a small town—especially to shop— in his life. Usually very small towns meant confinement and boredom. On top of that, his nice girl radar was spinning and squawking loudly in the back of his head, which meant either Kelly was really, really nice and he needed to steer clear, or somewhere under that appealing façade lay a much darker side waiting to spring out at him and shout *na na na na naner*. And yet, here he was eagerly awaiting his drive into the small town of Lawford with a nice girl.

"Any idea where you want to go?"

He shook his head. "Not really. Fiona said there are a handful of shoe and clothing stores that should be fully stocked this time of year." Now was a good time to let common sense kick in, steer clear, get what he needed, and meet up with his brother. The reason he came to New England in the first place. "You can drop me off at the start of Main Street and I'll walk my way through."

Kelly nodded and disappointment settled deep in his belly. Most likely, that darker side was about to show its colors.

A few moments later they came out from another curve along the narrow mountain road and the impact of wide open Main Street had his jaw dropping and Kelly muttering, "Oh wow."

The picturesque town was no doubt a colorful delight in the warmth of summer, but this winter wonderland was stunning. Arches of gold leafed holiday greetings extended up high from sidewalk to sidewalk. He suspected when the light switch was flipped after dark there would be more reason to stand in awe. Small colorfully painted brick buildings created splashes of contrasting color along a sea of pristine white snow. Even the street was packed tight with flat clean snow. Only the tire tread marks disturbed the white blanket. Small potted evergreens with dots of mostly red and gold ornaments lined the doorways.

"This is truly postcard perfect." In all his travels he could not remember seeing anything like it.

Kelly's gaze remained fixed on the street, her eyes sparkling with interest and perhaps a bit of awe. In some ways it was like watching an excited child's first glimpse of Santa Claus all decked out in his red velvet suit.

At the first available parking spot, Kelly pulled in and turned off the ignition. "This is as good a spot as any." Glenn thought she meant for him to start shopping, but she climbed out of the car, popped her trunk, pulled out a small black bag, threw it over her shoulder and slammed the trunk. "Shall we?"

Without waiting for an answer, she nimbly undid the zipper on the bag and retrieved a medium sized camera reminiscent of his old 35 millimeter he'd gotten from his grandfather on his thirteenth birthday. He was the only kid in his entire generation who had any idea what aperture was. He also had the best candid shots. Shots that a standard digital camera or phone simply couldn't capture. Which was probably why he'd been roped into working on the senior yearbook committee. At least until his dad was reassigned once again.

Lifting the camera, she began snapping away. From the rapid clicking, he could tell it was a digital camera. An expensive digital. Which made sense since she was a professional after all.

"This one is for long shots." She slipped the camera back into her bag and pulled out another smaller one. "And this," she pointed it at him and snapped, "is for lifestyle photos." At his lack of response, she added, "Closer, tighter shots. You'll see."

The very first shop had baskets of pinecones painted in an array of Christmas colors and dusting. Slowly, almost reverently, she lifted one into her hand. "My grandmother used to take me into the woods behind her house. We'd collect pinecones and then paint them. When she died and we cleaned out her attic, we found boxes marked by year with my name. In it was every pinecone we ever painted along with cards and other memories she obviously cherished."

"That's a lovely memory." He loved his grandparents dearly, but coming from a military family, there were no fond memories of holidays with doting grandparents.

She set the pinecone down and snapped a few close-ups. Another shop and more clicking of the shutter until they reached the first men's apparel store.

From the window he could see a wall of shoes and boots. "I see what Fiona meant."

To his surprise, rather than continue on her own, Kelly followed him inside. She marched straight to a pair of gray boots overflowing with fur trim, bulky beaded Velcro ties, and grinned. "Oh, these would be *so* perfect."

"For Alaska maybe."

"Come on." She grinned more widely. "A nice parka with matching fur trim. You'd be magazine cover worthy."

"Yeah." He smiled back. "Fish and Stream. *In Alaska.*"

The two chuckled loudly and when they'd left, she was the proud owner of a 'sweet' pair of red Tory Burch ballet flats marked down fifty percent and he wore a comfortable pair of black discreetly insulated snow boots. With traditional shoe laces.

By the time they'd reached the old church, they already had a long list of Main Street treasures to stop in and buy on the return stroll to the car.

"Perfect timing." From the front yard, Alan waved at his approaching brother. "We're just about to set up the nativity scene. Sorry, no hot glue or glitter involved," Alan teased, as he pulled his brother into a bear hug. "But figured since extra hands are always helpful, you wouldn't mind."

"At your disposal. What can I do?"

A tall man sporting a warm smile approached, arm extended. "I'm Pastor Bob. Nice to meet you. And Alan is right, extra hands are always appreciated."

"Perfect." One of the in-laws he'd met briefly last night after dinner smiled at him and held up a raw wooden board. "More hands?"

Glenn nodded. "Looks like it. Though you may regret it. My some-assembly-required skill was apparently handed off to my sister on the day God handed out talents."

Alan waved from his in-law to Kelly. "Kelly, this is my wife's brother-in-law Jake. He runs the local hardware store."

"Now all that lumber is making sense." Glenn smiled as if he'd figured out the solution for world peace.

"Except I'm merely helping carry the manger boards from storage." Jake shrugged.

Glancing down at a stack of boards already set to one side, Glenn wondered just how big a nativity scene were these people going to assemble? Proverbial sleeves rolled up, the entire group, including Kelly, hauled miscellaneous sized planks from the church basement to the front lawn space.

With the planks and trim pieces sorted by size, Jake gave a quick direction on assembly. "And most importantly, whatever you do, do not, I repeat, do not try to add the roof with only two sides up."

"That," Alan grinned at his in-law, "sounds like the voice of experience talking."

Chuckling, Jake rubbed the back of his head. "And I still have the bump to prove it."

Once the assembly had begun, the volunteers laughed, and teased, and for the first time in a very long time, Glenn could feel himself getting in the Christmas spirit. Once it became clear that there were actually two structures underway, Kelly switched from helper mode to professional photographer, capturing the process.

The first structure finished, Alan smiled and

nodded. "This looks great. Bet I could do something similar for a casual outdoor grill area. Protected from those rainy summer days." Still nodding and grinning and walking backwards for a better view, he teetered on the edge of the stone retaining wall.

"Careful." Glenn snatched hold of his brother's arm, stopping him from falling over onto the sidewalk.

"Or maybe not." Alan straightened his glasses, brushed at his sleeves and shooting a relieved glance at Glenn, thanked him.

Growing up, they'd always looked out for each other. Glenn had had his brother's back, siding with him when he'd told the family he wanted to try writing for a career, and Alan had been the one to keep Glenn thinking clearly through his divorce. Being together again for more than just a weekend wedding was nice. Hopefully the only thing they'd have to help each other through for a good long while would be putting this manger together. "You might want to stick to building stories."

Alan chuckled. "Agreed."

"So," Glenn glanced around, "are the statues still in the basement?"

"Statues?" the pastor repeated softly then smiled. "We don't use statues. We use people. In one hour shifts. And like the construction," the man slapped Glenn on the back of the shoulder, "we're always looking for volunteers."

"That I definitely would have to get a picture of," Kelly spoke through muffled laughter.

And why was it that he felt a strong need to volunteer just to keep her smiling at him?

CHAPTER FIVE

"These are seriously fantastic." Poppy sat at the edge of the massive island in the Hart family kitchen staring at Kelly's laptop screen.

With a small group gathered behind her, Kelly flipped from one photo to the next.

"Oh, my." Fiona moved her hand to her mouth in a poor attempt to hide her laugh.

"This is one of my favorites." Not wanting to draw too much attention to herself, she snuck a quick glance over her shoulder at Glenn. No reaction at all. She couldn't tell if he was a good sport and not reacting or annoyed and hiding it well. He and his brother had been working securing the roof of the manger when one of the grooves slipped and all the hay atop came tumbling down onto them. The next candid showed the utter shock on Glenn's face at being doused in hay. The expression had everyone giggling. Taking a second peek over her shoulder, she caught the glimmer of amusement in his eyes. Relief washed over her that he did indeed have a sense of humor. She'd have hated to find under that pleasant persona that a volcano of temper might suddenly erupt.

At all the laughter, Wooster's curiosity seemed to beat out the need for comfort. Contentedly curled at Lady's side, he lifted his rear, stretched his front paws, then trotted over and pawed at Glenn's leg.

"You're too big for me to lift."

Unaffected by the refusal, Wooster sat his rump down on the floor and leaning back, waved both paws in the air.

"Oh, that is so cute. I bet it never gets old." Fiona reached across the island and opening what looked like a cookie jar, pulled out a heart shaped treat. "Here you go, sweetie."

Tail wagging, the dog happily gobbled up the treat and the adult shenanigans forgotten, he made his way back to Lady, pawed at her until she shifted and then resumed his position snuggled beside her.

Something in Glenn's expression must have shown his concern at feeding the dog because Fiona smiled at him. "They're doggie treats. Lucy makes them into heart shapes so they look more like people cookies."

Poppy lifted her head, shifting her gaze from the screen to him. "The only heart shaped people cookies have icing on them. Otherwise, they're for Lady and Sarge. Or visiting pets."

"Got it."

Note to self. Be careful what you pilfer from the Hart cookie jars.

"Okay." Lucy slapped her hands together, rubbing them briskly. "We have a table to set, and dinner to get through. Tonight is the tree lighting ceremony and you do not want to miss this." She turned to Kelly. "I'm guessing that one of those cameras takes excellent night pictures?"

"Absolutely." She couldn't help grinning. She truly loved her work, and she prided herself on having some of the best equipment available, but today snapping candid shots of town, the decorations, the setting up of the manger, all of it, had been more fun than she'd had in an awful lot of years. She could hardly wait to discover what she could capture during tonight's trip to town.

"Perfect." Lucy stirred a large pot on the stove. "Guests take a seat in the family room. I'll call you as soon as dinner is ready. Everyone else, you know the routine."

Kelly closed the lid on her laptop. "I can help."

"Nonsense." Lucy shook her head. "In this house guests do not work." She chuckled a little. "At least not on your first full day."

Fiona Hart reached for a nearby apron on the hook by the back door. "Lucy is right. You two make yourself comfortable in the other room and dinner will be on the table shortly."

"Don't even think about arguing." Poppy held one hand up. "Trust me, many before you have been there done that. This will go much faster if you do as you're told."

"Yes, ma'am." Glenn gave a short salute. To Kelly's surprise, Lucy returned the salute.

Following him out the doorway and down the short hall, Kelly leaned in and softly asked, "Were you just being polite, or were you in the military?"

He chuckled. "Six years with Uncle Sam before I finally figured out I was not meant to follow in the family footsteps like my dad and grandfather."

"There's a lot of creative talent in your family for military brats."

"There is. Besides the obvious, Alan who writes, my sister paints. Not professionally, but that's her de-stresser. She can do anything. Still life, landscapes, she even did a fantastic portrait of her two kids."

"That's a lot of talent."

He nodded and came to a slow stop. "Wonder where she wants us to sit?"

"Do you suppose this is the wrong room?"

Boxes of Christmas paraphernalia were piled in

different corners of the room, some closed, some open. Another Christmas tree was up, but unlike the massive one in the foyer, this one was undecorated. Rows of garland were draped over the backs of chairs. Bags of popcorn ready to string, at least she figured that's what it was for, filled two chairs. Despite the clutter, the room evoked a sense of welcome enhanced by the glow from the roaring flames in a central fireplace.

"It will probably take longer for us to move this stuff than for them to set the table."

This time Kelly nodded. "I'm not sure I even want to try to move any of it. It may be in some special order or something."

Lucy came hurrying into the room. "So sorry. I can't believe I almost forgot this room looks like a warehouse." Moving faster than expected, she grabbed two of the boxes on the sofa, stuck them to one side on the floor, then brushed the seat cushions with her hand and with an almost queen-like wave, hurried back out the doorway and down the hall.

A stack of ornament boxes remained at one end of the couch.

"I guess it's the right room, and that's where we're supposed to sit." Glenn gestured to the vacant spots on the sofa.

For just a moment Kelly wondered if Lucy was up to something, or just overloaded with things to do for the holiday season. Considering all the decorations already around the house, both inside and out, she couldn't imagine what else could be in all these boxes.

Seated side by side on the sofa, Kelly had to admit, this assignment was turning out considerably easier than the butter freezer. Maybe she could talk her boss into another Lawford shoot in the summer. She could bookend the pitch from Memorial Day to Labor Day.

"Now, you're looking awfully serious."

"Sorry. Thinking about work."

"If it's the photos you've taken so far, they're fantastic. Really capture the spirit of the place."

"Thank you." Grabbing a nearby throw pillow from the floor, she cradled it in her arms and shifted to face him. "I was always the kid snapping pictures while everyone complained not again. Eventually though those same people would come back asking for copies, thrilled to have captured a precious moment of time on film. I freely admit I'm blessed to have been able to turn something I loved doing into a career. Speaking of career, I don't know what you do?"

"I guess we're a little alike. I was the only one of my siblings who didn't complain about piano lessons. In the beginning, to many a family member's chagrin, I would practice for hours and hours every day. Eventually my playing became less painful to everyone's ears. I loved playing the piano. If I was upset, playing made me happy, if I was happy, it made me happier, if I was tired, it rejuvenated me. Like you, I'm blessed to be able to make a living doing something I love."

"Oh, that would explain how you have so much time off for the holidays. I guess you get to decide which gigs you accept."

"Not exactly. I'm a—" Thirty pounds of dog bounded up and landed on his chest. "Wooster."

Within seconds, not one but both of the Golden's were on the sofa vying for a lap.

"Lady. Sarge," the General bellowed. The two dogs immediately jumped down and took their place at either side of their master. "Sorry about that. They should know better."

"Looks like Wooster is corrupting the troops." Glenn scratched at his dog's ear.

The General cleared a spot in a nearby chair and the conversation shifted to West Point. As much as she hated to admit it, all she could think was what a waste of low lights, a comfy sofa, a handsome man and a perfectly good roaring fire.

Glenn couldn't remember the last time he'd eaten so much. Well, the last time before last night and tonight.

"Leave the dishes for later." Lucy scurried about the kitchen pouring steaming chocolaty liquid into large thermos bottles and setting them one by one on the nearby counter. "There's plenty of warmth in a bottle. Two people per thermos."

Across the island, empty picnic baskets formed an assembly line. On a table on the other end, a pile of blankets were stacked. While they had enjoyed a delicious lasagna with cheesy garlic bread, the woman had been busier than a five star general the night before a major battle. If Lucy ever got the urge to open a restaurant she'd draw crowds from all the bordering states and beyond.

"I just love tree lighting night." Poppy grabbed a basket, stuck a thermos inside, a blanket, and her choice of snacks set out on the island as well. "We're going to meet up with Jake and Heather. This year he's not only cording off several spaces in front of the hardware store, he's going to fill the back of the pick up with hay and blankets and park it in front. We'll meet everyone there."

"Oh. I like that idea." Callie followed her sister in line, her husband holding the basket for her.

"He got the idea from Logan. Doesn't seem to be a shortage of pickup trucks in Texas."

His mind worked fast to put a name to a face. He was pretty sure Logan was Rose's husband.

"Are they coming tonight?" Callie asked.

"We are." Rose hurried in the back door. "Traffic was just insane. You'd think half of Boston was coming to Lawford."

"I wouldn't be surprised if they were. We have the best tree lighting night in the state."

Rose's smile spread even wider. "We really do. Even Logan thinks so, and you know Texans always think everything is better in Texas."

The cousins finished gathering up their baskets, someone handed him one filled to the brim. All the way out the door the chatter was loud, the smiles plentiful, and Glenn was beginning to better understand the appeal of living in Small Town USA for his brother.

He and Kelly had climbed into his brother's car when Lucy came running up. "The extra baskets are taking up almost all of the back seat of the General and Miss Fiona's Jeep. Got enough room for me?"

"Always." Cindy started to climb out of the front seat.

"No bother." Lucy waved her off. "I can squeeze in back here with Glenn and Kelly."

For once he didn't mind being squished in the middle of two people in the backseat. As a matter of fact, he rather liked it.

"This year is the biggest tree we've ever had. I can hardly wait to see it all lit up." Lucy chattered away the entire short ride into town. By the time they pulled up to the reserved spots in front of the hardware store, he knew all about the upcoming events. He also learned that one of the merry widows wasn't a widow, Floyd of Floyd's barbershop wasn't really named Floyd, and that Louise supposedly cheats at cards. Or was it Thelma?

Even before the car doors opened and everyone poured out, he could feel the energy sizzling in the air, heightened with the lilting sounds of Christmas carols playing from strategically placed speakers up and down the street. He had no idea how large the town was, but it sure looked like every one of them, young and old, had come out for the night. Some folks lined the streets in folding chairs, others sat on trunks or hoods of cars, a few remained standing, chatting and moving about amongst the others waiting for the light show.

"You okay?" Kelly asked.

"Me?" He jammed his thumb in his own chest.

"You look," she studied him a moment more, "distracted."

"Just thinking. I don't know if the West Coast has grown too crowded, too busy, to do things like this, or if I just need to get out more."

Kelly bit back a laugh. "I'm betting you get out plenty."

"Maybe, maybe not. Does leaving your house at night to go to work count as getting out?"

"Everything counts." She smiled up at him again. "If it makes you feel any better, I live in a city where the lighting of the Christmas tree is broadcast on national television, but this seems... bigger somehow." She shrugged. "This feels like a giant family reunion and it just happens to be someone's birthday too."

Glenn scanned the people nearby. Granted they were surrounded by Harts and Hart in-laws, but it was clear to anyone with eyes that just about everyone on the street knew each other. At least half the crowd had stopped to coo over Iris and Eric's little girl and her upcoming birthday before turning to the older two children and asking what they wanted for Christmas, if they'd been good for Santa, or some other equally meant-for-children holiday conversation. "I think you just hit the nail on the head. No matter where you turn the town manages to make you feel like everyone is one big family."

"A person would have to be Scrooge himself not to get caught up in the holiday spirit."

The music faded in the background, replaced with a strong, deep voice. "Welcome to Lawford's annual tree lighting. Please join me in the final countdown."

The announcement sent another wave of palpable anticipation through the crowd. If asked to testify in a court of law, Glenn might have to admit that Lawford could very well be the real Santa's Village in disguise.

As instructed, starting from ten and working their way down, the onlookers chorused the man's shouting out of numbers in reverse. When they got down to four, three, two, Glenn found himself shouting as loud and hard as the people around him and the click of Kelly's camera seemed to be keeping time with the raucous crowd. At the final shout of one, the tree lit up in a kaleidoscope of colors seconds before the silver streaked banners across Main Street followed suit in bright white lights that reminded him of shimmering stars.

Camera pointed at some of the Hart Land couples, Kelly snapped a few more candid photos before letting her camera hang loosely in front of her. "This tree is probably less than half the size of the one in New York, and the crowds a fraction as large, but this first day of Christmas festivities definitely beats the big city hands down."

There was no point in arguing, he agreed with her one hundred percent. He couldn't wait to see what the upcoming days had in store for him.

CHAPTER SIX

"Hello." Kelly struggled to open one eye and glance at the digital alarm clock. Still the middle of the night, it could only be one person calling at this hour. Her mother.

"Hello, dear. You don't sound very well. Catching a cold?" Clearly her mother had forgotten—again—that lunchtime in the Swiss Alps is not lunchtime on the American East Coast.

"I'm feeling fine, thank you. Just a little frog in my throat." Nothing two or three more hours of sleep followed by a hot cup of coffee wouldn't fix.

"The skiing has been simply marvelous. Everybody is just raving about the fresh powder."

Kelly's mother had always been a bit like that actress on the British sit-com who came from an ordinary blue collar family and yet aspired to be a pretentious aristocrat. Once Kelly's dad had passed on, her mother had shed the mantel of ex-wife and embraced the role of grieving widow. Meeting and marrying Carl a short time later gave her mother all the things she'd ever wanted. And a quaint family Christmas had never been one of them.

"Oh, and did I tell you that the new chef is simply to die for? The hotel finally cut ties with that sourpuss cook who considered himself a chef, and has a wonderful young man creating all sorts of mouth-watering treats. There's actually an irresistible chocolate martini for dessert made with, are you ready for this…"

Kelly snuggled into the pillow, pulled the blanket up over her shoulder, nodded, and grunted something her mother would consider sufficient to keep rattling on.

"Vanilla ice cream. Isn't that just deliciously decadent? There's still time for you to change your mind and join Carl and me for the holidays."

"Wish I could, but I have this story to shoot." It was the kindest thing she could say to a woman who had never cherished tradition or cared about celebrating with family. Kelly had spent one Christmas holiday with her mother and stepfather shortly after their wedding. Those two very long weeks were all she'd needed to know that jet setting in Europe was just fine for a fashion shoot but not terribly conducive to Rockwellian family portraits. Her own thoughts had her eyes popping open with surprise. Had that been what she'd wanted all these years? A return to the magical Rockwellian holidays of her youth before her parents divorced? Or had the thought merely been planted in her head after only a few days in a picture-perfect holiday setting?

"I have to run, Carl is famished. Say hi to your cousin for me."

"Will do." There was no point in reminding her mother that her Christmas plans had changed and she had no idea if the early shots would be enough or if she'd be stuck here through the New Year. Unlike her thoughts when she was first told her assignment would be in a real life Santa's Village, now she realized that being 'stuck' here most likely wouldn't be such an awful thing at all. She also realized that even though the sun wasn't even close to rising, the brief conversation with her mom had left her wide awake.

Even in a military family, she doubted anybody

at Hart house was awake at this early hour. Never mind ready for guests. She would have to settle for coffee from the small pot in her kitchen, and maybe a morning stroll with her camera. Already this little trip was reminding her of the joys of candid photography, a sharp contrast to her normally precisely staged world.

By the time the coffee had brewed, she was not only dressed and ready to start the day, she was actually excited to go strolling in the near pitch black of early morning. Camera around her neck and travel mug in one hand, she slipped the bright color pom-pom holding the key to the front door into her pocket. Out the door, she optcd to head up the hill toward the Hart House rather than down by the lakeshore. Layered in warm clothes, she figured staying away from the water would keep her comfortable.

Amazed at how well she could see, her path lit only by starlight and no moon, she wished she'd gone in the other direction when the rumble of an engine drew her attention toward the main house. A small white van with letters she couldn't quite make out rolled around toward the back drive and without thinking, Kelly lifted her camera and began snapping pictures of the van.

Moving faster then she'd planned, she cut right to circle around the house and hopefully capture the license plate of the vehicle and maybe even a driver. What she hadn't considered was what the heck would she do if she came face to face with a big burly guy carrying the Hart electronics out of the house. She hadn't even bothered to bring her phone with her. A lame choice regardless of the van. What if she were trapped by a bear, or fell in a cold creek. Most likely Hart Land had both.

The sound of the rear door slamming pushed

Kelly into action, moving around the van to the driver side opposite the Hart back door, her plan was to sneak around and snap a photo of the intruder as he went the other way toward the house. It was a solid plan, and she was rather proud of herself for thinking of it. Right up until the second she practically smacked into a petite woman who dropped a large bag and let out a slight shriek.

Kelly leapt back in retreat and forgot all about snapping a photo.

The petite person's hand flew to her chest and she squealed, "For the want of a four leaf clover, glory be you nearly scared ten years off me short life."

Me short life?

The woman squatted to retrieve the bag she'd dropped. "You're up awfully early for a houseguest. Having trouble sleeping, are you?"

"Sort of."

"Well, you might as well help me drop off Lucy's order. There's warm bread in here. Most people love it."

Warm bread sounded delicious. But the time? "Isn't it rather early for deliveries?"

"Not at Hart House. The General is an early riser, and sometimes Lucy likes to surprise him with some of my soda bread that he loves fresh out of the oven. Which I suppose I should be minding my manners. I'm Katie O'Leary."

"Kelly Chambers. Nice to meet you."

"Likewise. Now, follow me. I brought plenty for everyone. Mother always taught me there's no greater sin than running out of food. Well," Katie smiled impishly and bobbed her head sideways, "there might be one or two wee little other sins."

To Kelly's surprise, Lucy was in full cooking mode, with Mrs. Hart at her side.

"I brought one of your guests." Katie tipped her head in Kelly's direction. "And I took the liberty of bringing you some of my honey cinnamon butter."

Fiona Hart came up to the grinning baker and gave her a warm embrace. "You do spoil us, Katie."

"That's what I'm here for." The woman flashed a large toothy grin. A twinkle in her eyes told Kelly there was a great deal of truth in the petite woman's response. She also had the feeling there was more to that twinkle than merely being neighborly.

Fiona had already opened one of the two bags of warm bread, placed a slice on a plate, and was handing it to Kelly. "You'll have to try this. No one on the planet makes soda bread like Katie."

Eagerly, Kelly obliged taking a small bite, her taste buds instantly exploding with delight. "Oh my. I do believe you are right."

Fiona gently patted Kelly's shoulder. "Of course we are, dear. So tell us, what has you up so early this morning?"

"My mother called and woke me up. She forgets she may be in Switzerland, but the rest of the world most definitely is not."

Katie turned from pouring herself a cup of coffee to face Kelly. "A mother's love is an interesting thing. I wouldn't be holding it against yours that she can't tell time. I'm sure she loves you very much in her own way."

Another bite halfway to her lips, Kelly stopped to look Katie in the eye. The woman seemed so completely sure of what she just said that for the first time in many years, Kelly could almost believe that her mother really did love her more than Kelly realized. After all, she did call even if she was clueless about the time difference. Everything about this holiday season was bursting with new insight and now another colorful character to make these people's world truly a winter land of wonder.

One thing was sure, the crisp mountain air did wonders for a good night's sleep. Not till the sun shone brightly through his bedroom window and Wooster decided licking Glenn's face was an excellent way of communicating it was time for a walk, did he realize he'd overslept. The Hart family were early risers and Glenn had hoped to join them for breakfast. Actually, if he were a hundred percent honest with himself, what he really had hoped for was that Kelly would be at breakfast. At this late hour, he wasn't sure that would happen. Instead, he brewed a fresh pot of coffee while Wooster moseyed about the front of the cabin, sniffing and marking every shrub and plant, and then doubling back and repeating the ritual just in case another visiting canine should claim his territory.

Hungry enough for more than coffee, but not enough to actually cook, he dropped a couple of slices of bread in the toaster and opened a jar in the fridge that he was pretty sure was more of Lucy's homemade rhubarb jam. After he'd been fed and caffeinated, he would casually make his way up to the house. During snippets of overheard conversation the night before, there had been talk of gathering the troops. It had taken a few minutes for Glenn to realize they were talking about working on a float for tomorrow night's parade. His sister-in-law would have to be at the vet clinic but his brother intended to come this afternoon, as did a handful of other family members if jobs permitted. Though he expected many were going to come earlier to enjoy lunch by Lucy.

The sound of his cell phone ringing startled Glenn into spilling his coffee down his chin and shirt. He knew that cell phone and internet connections on the mountain ran the gamut from dismal to nonexistent. He'd grown so accustomed to the silence, that hearing his phone ring had been more than unexpected. "Hello?"

"Normally if someone answered the phone that way, I would say don't sound so surprised, but we all know that up here, having your phone ring is indeed not the norm. You must be standing by a window."

Glenn lifted his gaze from his meager breakfast to the large paned glass and the pretty snow-covered lake beyond. "Yep, little brother, sitting right in front of it."

"So what are you doing sitting down there and not up here helping?"

It wasn't that late. Glenn pushed away from the table and placing his cup in the sink, scanned the view from his cabin to Hart house. "Where are you? I don't see your car."

"That's because I'm parked by the barn a little ways up the hill from the main house. Lucy just dropped off a fresh batch of hot chocolate and mentioned you hadn't shown up for breakfast yet."

"Yet? Overslept a bit. Decided to eat in."

He could almost see his brother raising his brows and staring at the phone in disbelief, and who could blame him. Why would any sane person skip a breakfast buffet worthy of royalty to eat their own cooking. And in his case, it wasn't even cooking, it was toast.

"If you go to the main house," his brother continued, "I'll meet you there and bring you up. Compared to putting the manger together, the finishing touches on the float will be a piece of cake."

"On my way." He was all set to disconnect and

race out the door when his brain shifted into gear. "Wait. What about Wooster? Is it all right to bring him?"

"Of course. In this family, animals are almost more important than people."

By the time they'd all made it to the barn, he'd been surprised by how many Harts had turned out. Though he didn't know why it had surprised him. In the few days he'd been here, he'd been introduced to a large loving family whose world seem to revolve around the retired general, his sophisticated wife, and the big old rambling house complete with chattering housekeeper.

"Well, hello again."

Glenn turned to see Kelly squatting across the room, Wooster's front paws on her lap as she scratched behind his ears.

Her face turned and their eyes met. "Good morning."

Alan walked past them and muttered, "What's left of it."

"I've brought a round of fortitude." Lucy came through the large open barn doors carrying a tray of cheese and crackers and charcuterie.

"I'm going to need to buy a treadmill when I get home." Kelly pushed to her feet, gave the dog one last pat on the head, and followed Lucy to the table already heavily laden with foods of every shape and variety.

"Someone pass me the hot glue gun, please." Callie stood on a ladder atop the Hart Land Inn float.

Wow. When these guys made a float they didn't mess around. For some reason he'd expected homemade floats to be a small trailer with some cotton batting for snow and maybe a blowup Santa, but not this. Especially a float not officially entered for judging.

"Isn't it impressive?" Hands on her hips, Kelly looked up at the sparkling star atop what might be a 10 foot fully decorated Christmas tree. The backdrop was no less impressive, a fireplace surrounded by bookcases set the perfect scene for all the large boxes wrapped in front of the tree. "Mrs. Hart is a master bow maker."

He nodded. "More than impressive."

"Here you go." Poppy hurried up the steps onto the main portion of the float and reached up, handing her sister what she'd asked for, then faced Kelly. "You should mention that to Grams. She'd like hearing it."

"Thanks, sis." Callie proceeded to attach velvet bows strategically along the top of the tree.

Brushing her hands along her denim clad thighs, Kelly swallowed her last bite of brie on a cracker and faced Glenn. "Apparently our job this afternoon is to make sure everything placed on the float is secure against wind and movement."

"Makes sense."

The trailer had to be at least twenty, maybe thirty feet long. Long enough for six people to roam back and forth, handing each other different pieces or refilling glue guns, or occasionally making an executive decision and moving a piece from one spot to another.

Somehow, Kelly and Glenn had been placed on sprinkle duty. Tasked with making sure everything sparkled from one end to the other, Glenn sprayed small sections of the cotton covered floor with special fabric glue and Kelly hand sifted the silver and gold sparkles onto the freshly applied glue spot. The first try, more sparkle had landed on them than the float. Next attempt had been too sparse, but little fell on them. Another try and shiny pieces poured out too thick, creating small clumped mounds.

"We'll get the hang of it." Kelly smiled up at him, holding the container of sparkles the size of a parmesan cheese jar. "I'll shake more slowly."

"Sounds like a plan." He sprayed, she shook, and this time the sparkles seemed more scattered. "I think we're getting the hang of it."

"I think we are." Her grin grew wider. "I don't think I've had this much fun with art supplies since kindergarten."

"Reminds me of my mother."

"Really?" She paused jar in hand. "How so?"

"Moving around all the time with few friends and even less family around, Christmas wasn't a big deal around our house. Still, every year Mom tried to do something special for each kid just for the season. Apparently I was the only one who had inherited the Christmas gene. So she and I would make the designated something special together every year, and no matter what it always involved lots of glue and lots of glitter, so you might say this is my calling in holiday times."

"Sounds like fun. What kind of things did you make?"

"One year it was personalized placemats." He should find it.

"Ooh, fun *and* practical."

"When you're raising kids on a budget, most splurges needed to be practical too. Even when they turned out rather funny." He felt his cheeks pull at the memory. "Mom was great. She never tried to correct my not so precise efforts. I think I actually still have mine in a box somewhere."

"Why in a box?"

"After the army, like a typical bachelor, unpacking stuff I didn't use seemed rather unnecessary. Then when I got married my wife didn't have a whole lot of need for anything that didn't fit her lifestyle."

Kelly winced softly. He should have reacted the same way, but at the time he'd been so blinded by who he thought Amanda was that losing himself to her agenda had been easy.

"Anyhow, eventually that blew up in my face, so after the separation, I rented the apartment on the opposite coast, sight unseen, ordered what little I had, including the boxes Mom had given me, delivered before the ink on the divorce papers was dry, and the military brat in me still hasn't gotten around to unpacking it all." He wasn't about to tell her that it simply had never occurred to him that he should try to make his apartment into a home.

Having gotten the hang of it now, Glenn shared stories of his mom's cookie baking efforts, including the ones that served better as door stops. He was halfway through the tales of the homemade holiday stockings that wound up in all sorts of assorted shapes and sizes, none of which resembled the original patterns, when Kelly tripped over a raised electric plug and teetered backward. Dropping the can to the floor, Glenn reached out just in time to save her from falling off the edge.

The only problem was that he now held her firmly in the fold of his arms, close enough to know she used vanilla shampoo, and fit perfectly against him. His brain stuttered in neutral and giving no thought to the consequences, he leaned forward, eager to see if her kiss was as sweet as her perfume.

A crash sounded from the opposite corner of the barn, snapping his brain out of neutral and into reverse before he could find his answer.

"Wooster!" Closest to the scene of the crime, Poppy bolted to the dog's side and scooped him into her arms.

He and Kelly were only a few short steps behind

her. He could see blood dripping from one paw and hoped dogs were like people and the amount of blood from a finger or paw wounds was not indicative of severity.

Alan came up beside them. "I know a good vet."

"I don't know." Now that he had a better view of the paw, a small wave of relief filled him. "The cut looks pretty superficial. Just a nick."

A pained expression on her face, Kelly gently patted Wooster's rump. "We should probably still have Cindy make sure there's no glass in the cut."

"I've had lots of kids do dumb things." Callie came up to them and quickly examined the paw. "I think Glenn might be right. If it's a clean cut we can rinse it off and see before we run off to Cindy's."

Lucy stood over the mess the dog had made. Broken glass, scattered ornaments, and miscellaneous unused decorations were strewn across the corner of the floor. "Uh, oh." She bent over and turned back to face them, half a pinecone in her hand. "If he's eaten the other half, forget cleaning the wound. Someone should take him straight to Cindy. Now."

CHAPTER SEVEN

The tone in Lucy's voice had everyone snapping to attention. Kelly grabbed a roll of paper towels from the table and as Glenn walked briskly toward the door, she hurried beside him, wrapping the dog's paw to stem the bleeding.

The first thing that came to mind was whether or not pinecones were toxic. She knew dogs chewed on sticks and other things in nature to sharpen their teeth or aid their digestion without causing them any harm. On the other hand, she also knew some foods like chocolate and raisins could kill a dog. But she knew nothing about pinecones. Especially painted pinecones.

As tough and battle trained as Callie appeared from her years of teaching high school, Poppy was the flip side of her sister, delicate, gentle, and right now looking more nervous about the dog than any of them. "I hope this isn't like chocolate."

Lucy shook her head, hurrying beside them. "Pinecones aren't toxic."

An audible sigh of relief could be heard from every person within earshot.

"The problem," Lucy continued, "is that like chicken bones they can splinter and cause blockages, perforations, and other unpleasantries."

The relief of a moment ago was short lived. Out the door, Kelly realized she'd been the last one to arrive and now blocked the other cars. She was glad for an excuse to go with them. "I'll drive."

"Do you know where you're going?" Alan asked.

Kelly nodded. "Yes. I saw the clinic the other day when we were in town. I can find it again."

Holding the passenger door of her car open for his brother, Alan pulled his cell from his pocket. "Good. I'll call Cindy and let her know you're coming. I won't be far behind."

With a nod, Glenn climbed into the car. Kelly turned the ignition, backed out, and they were on their way.

"You can breathe now," he said softly.

"What?"

"You look like you're holding your breath. You're also squeezing the steering wheel so tightly you might snap it." One corner of his mouth lifted in a nervous smile.

She could see the worry glistening in his eyes, and yet he was trying to reassure her. How sweet was that? Taking in a deep breath, she blew it out slowly and stretched her fingers about, easing her hold on the wheel. "I just wish he'd stolen another shoe instead."

This time both sides of Glenn's mouth lifted in a more steady smile. "Don't let him hear you. He might take that as permission to commit another crime against Jimmy Choo."

She glanced briefly at the dog content in Glenn's arms and for the first time since the boxes came crashing down, felt like smiling. "At least he doesn't look like he's in pain."

"I was thinking the same thing. It's probably the only reason I'm not losing my sh…stuff."

"I may have to rethink the rethinking getting a dog thing."

He chuckled. "Run that by me again."

"I've always thought that dogs and apartments don't mix. Especially in a concrete city like New York. Only, Wooster is so cute—even if he did eat one of my favorite shoes—that he had me rethinking maybe getting a very small dog. Now I'm not so sure I'm cut out for parenting of any kind."

"You seem to be doing fine so far." His smile was still there, nice and steady. "And there probably aren't many barns with boxes of old ornaments in New York City for a small dog to get into."

She heard herself sigh. "There isn't very much of anything like here in New York City. I mean yes, we have the tree at Rockefeller Center, and a carriage ride through the park under a blanket can be fun, even the chestnuts roasting on street corners are a treat, but somehow after seeing all that the town is putting into the holiday, those things seem so impersonal."

"I know what you mean." His smile slipped. "I've got a couple more weeks vacation time and already I think I'm going to miss this picturesque town."

She knew exactly what he meant, only she didn't think—she knew.

Of all the things Glenn had thought he might do with Kelly this afternoon, a ride to the vet with Wooster had not been one of them.

"It's going to be all right." Now she was the one reassuring him. Or maybe she was just convincing herself. Either way, it was obvious to anyone with eyes that she'd come to care for the dog too.

"Here we are." She pulled more sharply into the parking space then she probably should have.

To Glenn's surprise, Cindy herself came rushing out the door. "What have we got here?"

Quickly, Glenn explained in more detail what Alan had told his wife over the phone.

"Do you think it's serious?" Kelly followed them into the building and down the hall to the first exam room.

Cindy already had her stethoscope in her ear, was listening to the dog breathe, and held one finger at Kelly, letting her know that she would answer shortly. Removing the ear buds and draping the stethoscope around her neck, Cindy palpitated the dog's abdomen. A loud, hollow thunking sound echoed in the small room.

Done with the remainder of the examination, Cindy scratched under Wooster's chin. "Honestly, everything sounds fine. Though he does have quite a bit of gas."

Kelly's mouth hung slightly open. "You can tell he has gas?"

"It's pretty easy." Cindy held out two fingers of her right hand and gently tapped them on the two fingers of her left hand. "Same principle works on dogs and people. When you slap your fingers together on the abdomen it should make a very flat sound. When you hear a deep hollow sound, that's usually gas. Of course I'm looking for other things as well, but those are the two simplest and most common things you hear when palpitating the abdomen."

Glenn nodded and waited for the other shoe to fall.

"Wooster has already avoided the first problem with eating something like a pinecone, which is an obstruction causing him to choke. Whatever he ate has made it to the next step."

Once again, Glenn nodded. "So now what?"

"Now we do an x-ray and see what's going on inside. That will determine whether we have to go in and do surgery or simply wait for nature to run its course."

"Nature?" Kelly repeated.

"Best case scenario will be for this little guy to just poop out what he can't digest." Cindy's expression remained unreadable as she lifted the dog off the table into her arms. "This won't take long. Wait for me here."

As Cindy carried his dog into the hall, Alan came walking in from the opposite direction. The two stood face to face just outside the door. "Any news yet?"

Except for the light in her eyes at the sight of her husband, Glenn still couldn't read Cindy's face to determine if this situation was more or less serious than she was making out.

"You two look like someone stole all your Christmas presents." Alan strode all the way into the room. "I happen to know from a reliable source, the lady's really good at what she does."

"I don't doubt that at all." Glenn's gaze remained on the now empty hallway outside. "I don't understand why the dog is returning to his puppyhood with all this chewing."

Alan shrugged. "Probably a little stressed from being away from home. Hopefully he won't get the urge to gnaw on anything else the rest of your stay here."

His gaze hadn't left the doorway when a warmth covered his arm. Kelly had inched closer to him and rested her hand on his forearm. The touch was surprisingly reassuring, and welcome. He wasn't sure what to make of it other than he liked it, and that was not a good thing. He didn't do like anymore. Like was one step away from love and he didn't do that anymore either. Even if it was the woman who was clearly very worried about the welfare of the dog who'd eaten her favorite shoes. How sweet was that?

"We might as well sit down." Alan sat on the bench against the wall.

Neither Glenn nor Kelly budged until Cindy came walking back into the room.

This time a smile graced her face. "Wooster is going to be fine."

Kelly squeezed his arm and Glenn had an overwhelming urge to pull his sister-in-law into a huge hug and then turn and kiss Kelly, and not necessarily in that order.

"Thank you." He figured simply expressing his gratitude was the safer call. "Now what? We watch the poop?"

"Actually." Her smile shifted to a light chuckle. "I didn't see any sign of anything resembling pinecone shards. Keep an eye on him just in case, but I think it's safe to say he's in the clear."

"That's wonderful news." Kelly beamed.

Alan waved his arms in the air, palms up. "Told you she was the best."

"You're biased." Cindy leaned over and gave her husband a quick peck on the lips. "Let me finish the paperwork and the vet tech will bring Wooster out."

"Thank you again," Glenn repeated.

Her hand still on his arm, Kelly faced him. "I think this would be a good time to find the ladies room. I'll be right back"

Glenn nodded, immediately missing the warm touch as she pulled away.

His brother's hand landed on his shoulder. Standing behind him, Alan kept his gaze fixed in the same direction as Glenn's. "She's not Amanda."

"I know that."

"Do you?" Alan shifted to his side. "The two of you looked like a couple of first time parents worrying together over your kids first fall."

"I just met her. We're practically strangers."

"Key word there is practically, bro." Alan patted his shoulder again. "Trust me when I say you guys don't look anything like strangers."

"What's this box doing in the kitchen?" Fiona Hart sifted through the miscellaneous decorations in the cardboard box on the kitchen table.

Standing at the sink, Lucy chopped carrots for tonight's dinner and barely glanced over her shoulder. "It's from the barn. The leftovers from the float."

Thoughts of how her family coming together at the barn to work on the float the last few months had Fiona's cheeks tugging at her lips. "That float is looking good. The General is going to make a wonderful Santa."

"That he is." Lucy nodded in agreement. "I think we've outdone ourselves this year. I like it even better than the year of that big castle."

"Oh, that was a nice float, but I never did understand what Cinderella's castle had to do with Christmas. Though the important thing to remember is that the children loved the float that year." Fiona pulled out one of the pinecones from the bottom of the box. "Are these the pinecones Glenn's dog got into?"

Still working over the sink, Lucy casually peeked over her shoulder. "I guess so."

Something in Lucy's nonchalant response set

Fiona's internal alarm on high alert. There were several old pinecones clustered at the bottom of the box with some candle holders, ornaments, and stuffed toys that had not been used on the float. She weighed a full spray-painted pinecone in one hand, but stared at the sliced pinecone in the other. For a different project last year, George had sliced several pinecones carefully down the middle, and just for the heck of it, she'd tossed the leftovers into the supply box for decorating the float. "Didn't Poppy say that Wooster had eaten half a pinecone?"

This time Lucy didn't bother looking over her shoulder she merely nodded. "I believe she did."

When Lucy would not look Fiona in the eye, there was always a reason. And unfortunately it was rarely good, and almost always had to do with some matchmaking scheme. Without proof, she wasn't going to make a fuss, but she supposed, if she was right, on the grand scheme of things, pretending a dog had eaten half a pinecone so two people would ride alone in the car to the vet's office was much safer than locking two people in a walk-in freezer. At least she hoped so.

CHAPTER EIGHT

The last couple of days had been spent helping the Hart family wherever extra hands or wheels were needed. Since the General and Mrs. Hart were the head of the Winter Festival committee, most of the focus had been on the final details preparing for today's kick off of the town's biggest fair of the year. Since Lawford apparently hosted quite a few throughout the year, that made this event rather massive for coordination and execution.

Every weekend starting today until Christmas, the church parking lot and a portion of the back field would host booths of food and crafts and everything conceivable for Christmas and New Years. The entire event would be entertained by traditional carolers dressed in Dickens era clothing, and of course the required St. Nick checking off his list whether the children of Lawford Mountain had been naughty or nice. This evening, as part of opening day, there would be the parade of floats the town had been looking forward to since last Christmas. Other events would be dispersed over time, culminating in the Christmas Pageant. Another event that half the town appeared to be involved in, including Iris' two children, both senior angels, wings and all.

All of which was very exciting, except Glenn had gotten little sleep the last two nights checking hourly on Wooster, just in case the vet had missed something. His head knew that his sister-in-law was an excellent veterinarian and would not have overlooked anything, but his heart didn't want to cooperate and worried about the dumb mutt anyway. Adding to his already established lack of sleep, last night had been a marathon effort at completing the pageant costumes in time for this afternoon's dress rehearsal. Glenn had learned more about angel wing making in the last twenty-four hours than he ever thought possible. After breakfast this morning, he had fallen deep and soundly asleep on the living room sofa with a very sleepy Kelly at his side.

"Rise and shine." Lucy came into the room more cheerfully than any human being up all night with glue guns and sewing machines had a right to. "Sorry to have to wake you, but the General and Miss Fiona left hours ago for the fair grounds but missed this last load of costumes. Your car seems to be the only one available to run these over to the church in time for dress rehearsal. Would you mind?"

"Hours?" Glenn glanced at his watch and swallowed a groan. Bad enough he'd dozed off, but to have been asleep for hours on his hosts' sofa was more than a little embarrassing.

"No. Not at all." Kelly straightened, stretching her arms and turning her neck. "I think Marine boot camp might have been easier than last night."

"Hardly." Lucy chuckled shaking her head.

"Remind me to never make fun of kids with lopsided halos and bent wings again." Kelly stood, hands on her hips, tipping at the waist to her left then right.

"You go to a lot of children plays, do you?"

Her face crinkled as she twisted to one side of the other. "Not really, but last year at my cousin's home we attended the little production at their church. Nothing as big as here, but the two little angels both had catawampus halos and I don't believe either of the wings made it intact through the duration of the play."

"Duly noted." Extending his arm toward the boxes neatly stacked to the side of the couch, he wondered how this woman looked so sweet and so beautiful even with cushion creases on her cheek. "Shall we?"

"Lets."

It only took a few minutes to load the two boxes into Kelly's car, but the short drive to town was slowed by the number of tourists coming and going. With most of the parking lot taken up by the massive tents, a few reserved parking spaces were for the people who still had to come and go during the day.

Kelly pulled into the only vacant space. "Sure is a good thing most of the locals walk wherever they have to go this time of year or we might be parking in the next town and carrying the boxes in."

"Amen to that." Not that he was very sure that his choice of words was appropriate considering where they were standing and where they were going, but he was pretty sure in light of the season God would forgive him.

"Ooh. Just in time." Smiling as usual, Poppy came out from behind her desk and waved a hand for them to follow her. "The children should be here any minute."

As they passed the pastor's office, he too rose from behind his desk and came into the hall to greet them. "We really appreciate you helping the General and Miss Fiona. I don't know what this town would ever do without them. I don't think there's a resident that doesn't consider them like their own grandparents."

Kelly nodded. "I've only been here a few days

and yet I understand exactly how you feel."

The pastor turned in the same direction as Poppy. Both Glenn and Kelly followed, depositing the boxes beside the other costumes. "If you're not in a hurry, we would love to have a real audience to test the performance on, besides the parents."

He looked to Kelly, she half shrugged and turned to the pastor. "Do you think the parents would mind if I took some photographs? Of course we would get releases if we chose to publish any of them."

With a grin as wide as Main Street, the pastor shook his head. "There might be one or two parents who are a tad camera shy, but my guess is most will be flaunting their children at the chance of having them in a magazine publication."

A petite older woman with large streaks of gray hair came hurrying down the hall. "Oh Lordy Lord. I do think this will be the biggest crowd we've ever had."

The pastor leaned into Glenn and very softly whispered, "Nancy says that every year."

On his other side, Poppy leaned in, hardly covering her mouth with her hand, and whispered, "And I'm pretty sure she's been doing this since before I was born."

It only took Glenn a few minutes to realize *this* meant playing the piano for the pageant.

Introductions were quickly made and the woman continued on her way, delighted with the prospect of a massive turnout. Pastor Bob directed them down a different hall through a pair of double doors. "The main church suffered a fire earlier in the year, and thankfully the town and the church, with a little help from a generous patron, managed to have the old building restored to its original glory. But when these old churches were built hundreds of years ago they didn't anticipate a yearly pageant with the entire town attending. Especially a town the size of Lawford now. Before I arrived, this hall was added on. It's mostly used for reception and community parties, but this time of year it allows us to handle overflow from services and of course—"

"The pageant," Glenn finished the sentence for the man beaming with pride over his small church and the community it supported.

Over a card game the other night, he and Kelly had been updated on most of the town's history. Including how Pastor Bob had only joined them a couple of years ago after the previous pastor had been transferred to another parish. Everything was on the up and up, but Thelma—or was it Louise— one of them was convinced the poor pastor had requested a transfer as a reprieve from Lucy's challenging matchmaking efforts.

Having taken a moment to run out to her car, Kelly now stood camera in hand.

"Do you carry that everywhere you go?"

"Always." Fidgeting with something on the camera, she hadn't bothered to look up. Finally having it set exactly the way she wanted, she lifted her gaze to meet his. "This camera is as much a part of me as my hands and feet. When I look through the lens, it allows me to tune out everything around me, all the craziness in the world, and focus on the one thing that has captured my eye. No matter how insane life gets, the simplicity of one thing never ceases to amaze me."

Had he sat somewhere a month ago and the person beside him had said exactly that, he would have thought they were crazy, but looking into sparkling emerald green eyes, he knew exactly how she felt.

"Oh my gosh." Kelly held up the cutest keychain with strings of beads and larger hard shelled objects painted in different colors. "What are these?"

The woman seated behind the booth reached into a bowl beside her and lifted a handful of ordinary brown pecans. "This is how they began."

Dangling from her fingers, Kelly studied the shiny slick colors. How could it be?

"I got the idea on a cruise once. A street vendor had all sorts of fun jewelry and key chains and a few things I never did quite figure out. I kept thinking there had to be a substitute close to home for the natural seeds and nuts the island folks used. Eventually I found that pecans worked best. Different trees give different shapes. Some are long and narrow, others almost round. But it can't be done with the easy to peel paper thin nuts. That's just a mess waiting to happen."

Kelly thought of all the time she'd gone fishing in her handbag looking for her car keys and come up empty, finally dumping the contents out only to find the keys tucked in a corner somewhere. For years she threatened herself with buying a large colorful pom-pom like the ones on the cabin key, so she could spot her keys from across the room, but one of these would make a much more artistic substitution. When her gaze fell on a row of similar dangling key chains attached to carabiners instead, the decision was made. She got a favorite one for herself, and a few more for friends and family.

Across the aisle, Glenn and his brother were lost in conversation at a small table displaying hand carved chess pieces. Interestingly, the thing that caught Kelly's attention wasn't the beautiful workmanship, it was the casual way Alan and his wife Cindy held hands. Discreetly lifting her camera, she snapped a shot of the gesture. Their grip wasn't fully entwined, but rather a few fingers looped together. Each moved about looking at different pieces, but always remaining within arm's length and never letting those two fingers separate. So casual and yet so telling. A comfortable connection that neither wanted to sever. It might be foolish holiday sentimentality, but not even in Paris, the city for lovers, had she felt such a strong longing to connect with someone. Her gaze shifted to Glenn holding up a beautiful walnut colored knight. Even from where she stood she could see the delicate detail carved on the horse's head.

Handing the piece back to the craftsman, Glenn nodded. "I'll take this set, please."

Only one aisle perused and already they were laden with multiple bags of goodies. At the end of each aisle in a perpendicular formation, table after table of edible delights, many boasting having come from old family recipes, summoned Kelly to try them all. An impossible task that she was sorely tempted to accomplish.

"Are you thinking what I think you're thinking?" Glenn handed the attendant behind the table a dollar and lifted a cookie. "If these taste anything like the spitzenbubens Lucy served the other night, this could be the best dollar I've ever spent."

Not quite tasting the treats at every table, they'd turned the corner on another aisle when a pair of wayward children dressed like Santa's elves came barreling up the aisle, parting the shopping crowds like Moses had the Red Sea. Except one kid in particular seemed awfully nimble on his feet and whizzed past Kelly, so close and so fast, he had her spinning in place and almost tumbling into Glenn's arms. "So sorry."

"We really should stop meeting this way." His eyes twinkled with amusement at the tired old cliché and reference to her falling in the barn. Carefully helping her regain her balance, his hands slowly slid down her arms, but he made no attempt to step back and put distance between them. Instead a now intense gaze remained fixed on her face, and she would almost be willing to bet a year's salary his gaze remained more specifically on her lips. Would it be the end of the world as she knew it if she stepped into his personal space in anticipation of a kiss? One hand had paused at her wrist, then his thumb gently drew swirls along the side of her hand. She might have taken a half step closer, or maybe not. She wasn't completely sure.

"Kelly? Is that you? Kelly?"

Hating to break the connection, she turned slightly in the direction of the voice.

"That *is* you." Through the crowds, a face came into view.

"Jeremy, this is a surprise."

"And the last place I'd have expected to bump into you. Not your usual stomping ground." Jeremy had been at the magazine longer than she had. His food column had become quite popular and both his name and face had become easily recognizable up and down the east coast.

"I'm doing a holiday spread. You know, Rockwellian holiday is alive and well. What brings you here?"

"You think I'd miss the best food festival east of the Rockies?"

"That good?" Her instinct had been to take a step back, put some distance between her and Glenn and the almost exchange. Maintain her professional demeanor in front of her colleague. Except that same hand that had so gently caressed her own, had now firmly encircled hers in his and held on with a very protective grip.

"The best." Jeremy's gaze redirected over her shoulder and settled on Glenn, before he shot his hand out. "Jeremy Heins. Nice to meet you."

Still holding on tightly with one hand, Glenn shook the proffered hand with his other. "Glenn Peterson."

The way the two men seemed to stare each other down, if she didn't know that Jeremy was happily married, and Glenn was nothing more than a friend, she'd have sworn the two were having a pissing contest over her.

"Small town New England isn't your usual territory to cover." Jeremy nodded and retreated half a step. "I think I understand. Now."

Glenn returned the half nod and Kelly looked at the two men. Now she was seriously confused. "It's not—"

"There you are." Jeremy's wife Carol came up behind him holding up a similar keychain to the one Kelly had bought. "One minute you were right beside me and the next you were gone."

Jeremy slung his arm around his wife's waist. "Sorry, hon. Look who I ran into."

"Kelly. Hello." The woman's dissatisfaction with her husband slid away behind a bright smile. "Isn't this a nice surprise."

"She was sent here on," Jeremy cleared his throat, "assignment."

"To cover a traditional holiday season." Kelly felt the need to correct what Jeremy was implying.

The innuendos went right over Carol's head. "Isn't it just perfect. Back in the city there are plenty of little boutiques—"

"Expensive boutiques," her husband filled in.

Carol waved him off. "Plenty of boutiques and storefronts and decorations and holiday mirth, but it's all buried in big city trappings. This," her arm made a grand gesture around her, "is apple pie American."

That was as good a description as any she'd thought of so far. "Well, we really need to move on. I am still working."

"Right." Jeremy nodded, a stupid smile on his face. "Working."

Kelly resisted the knee jerk reaction to roll her eyes and argue. She figured that would just fuel the fire.

"For the record," he addressed Glenn, "it's about time some guy smartened up and snapped her up."

"Jeremy!" his wife smacked his arm.

"What?" The man looked truly confused.

Carol shook her head and sighed. "Just ignore him. I think someone spiked the eggnog. You two have a nice festival. And you," she turned to Kelly, "don't work too hard."

Forcibly turning her husband around, Carol nudged him back down the aisle and waved cheerily over her shoulder at Kelly and Glenn as they disappeared into the crowd.

Now all Kelly needed was a nice big rock to crawl under. Could she feel any more embarrassed? Nothing like having a coworker wave your love life—or lack of one—out in the open for all to see. Especially one person in particular. One person in particular who was still, very firmly, holding her hand.

CHAPTER NINE

There was only one thing that had happened in the last few minutes that Glenn was sure of—he didn't want to let go of Kelly's hand. He felt like a kid crushing on the new girl in school, and tripping over his own hormones in the process. When that man walked up to Kelly with so much familiarity, it took everything in Glenn not to scoop her up and carry her someplace far away from any competition for her attention. Of course the whole idea was ridiculous. The man was harmless, and Glenn had no right to behave so possessively.

He might feel like a teenager, but he was a grown man with a good head on his shoulders, and the manners his mother had taught him. Breathing in and out, nice and slow, he raised their laced fingers in front of them. "Is this okay?"

Time seemed to stand almost still for the fraction of a moment it took for her to nod her head. The teenager in him bounced back to life, ready to grin like a fool and prance around the fairgrounds showing off the prettiest girl in town. The grown man with a good head on his shoulders settled for a soft smile and another hour or so of shopping.

Somewhere between the needlepoint Christmas stockings that cost way more than any reasonable person should have paid, but he knew his sister would absolutely adore, and the apron with *Don't Get Your Tinsel In A Tangle* embroidered across the front for his grandmother, they'd stopped at the games corner. Grown men tossed candy cane painted horseshoes with the seriousness of an Olympic competition. Iris and Eric's niece and nephew had challenged Kelly and him to a game of corn hole.

Kelly carefully aimed, gently swung her arm, and let the bag sail across to the wooden board. Despite her effort, the bag slid over the top and onto the ground.

"At least you got it on the board this time." Glenn walked beside her, retrieving the four bags.

"I suppose. But I still think corn hole is a silly name for this."

In all his years growing up across the globe with his military family, he'd missed that the outdoor game of pitching bean bags onto a wooden board with holes cut out was called corn hole.

Clutching her four bags against her chest, Emily crossed back to her spot for the next round. "Uncle Eric says it's because the bean bags used to be filled with corn not beans. So the goal of the game is to get the corn in the hole. I guess they got lazy and shortened it to corn hole."

"That actually makes sense. Thank you Emily." Kelly leveled her gaze with his and he could read the same thought running through his mind in her eyes. Outsmarted by a little kid.

By the time the sun was setting and the colored lights illuminated the tree and street decorations, everyone in the family had migrated to meet up at the same spot in front of the hardware store on Main Street for the parade. Jake had lined up chairs on the edge of the curb. This way the folks behind them could still have a nice view. Surrounded by coolers and decorated with balloons and noisemakers, Glenn couldn't imagine how much more these people did for New Years.

"This is sort of exciting." Kelly leaned forward in her chair, camera in hand, watching the growing crowd around her, she continued to click away.

"Look." Glenn pointed down the street. The front of the first float was just barely in their line of sight.

Iris's kids did an anxious dance around her and her husband. In contrast, the young one sitting on her lap who Glenn would have expected to be overflowing with energy, remained perfectly still, thoroughly fascinated by the people and colorful paraphernalia crossing his path.

Despite the vast amounts of colored lights sparkling overhead, the stars above were still bright and plentiful. "Looks like the weathermen are wrong again."

Lucy shook her head, making a tsking sound. "I find the best philosophy is to simply do the opposite of what forecasters tell you. If there's expected sunshine, bring an umbrella. They'd been threatening us with ice storms for the past couple of weeks and I've yet to see more than a few flurries."

"I'm not going to argue with you. I'm always expecting clear skies promised by the weatherman, only to find myself outside caught in a downpour with my umbrella in my desk drawer." Callie lifted her head to the sky. "Definitely glad the forecasts are off again."

Overhead, the music shifted from lighter traditional holiday music to tunes with more of an upbeat. From where Glenn sat he could already see the enthusiasm rising in the crowd as toes began tapping to the tunes. Little kids waved wands of pink or blue cotton candy. It wasn't long before the first of the floats eased its way down the street.

Leading the way, the Hart float rolled along. The General wore his costume well. The man really did look like the well loved Santa Claus and the sparkles shimmered under the street lights exactly as everyone had hoped. An unexpected sense of pride surged as the float grew closer. He'd done so little to help and yet, he had helped.

So many aspects of living in a small town were starting to make sense to him. Especially why his award-winning author of a brother, a person used to living in big cold cities, had stepped into life in small-town USA, and never looked back.

The day had been amazing. Kelly had never been much of a shopper, but today she'd been torn between all the fun finds and the need to capture every bit of it on camera. Seeing the Hart family float making its way up Main Street after having spent time and elbow grease helping, had been the piece de resistance. Much more of a thrill than she had expected. Another added kick to the fun of watching the other floats roll by had been knowing the people involved in each one. All the old jokes and clichés about small towns had proven true in so many ways. In her short stay at the Inn, she'd met a slew of people and not a one felt like a stranger. There was no mistaking the float that represented Floyd's barbershop. Besides the traditional red, white, and blue barber pole dead center and draped in seasonal garland, she was pretty sure the two mannequins in uniform, except for the red and white Santa hats, were supposed to be Sheriff Andy Taylor and his deputy Barney Fife. Then of course there were the two barber chairs, each with a waving elf.

The other float that had her laughing out loud carried the merry widows. The card playing women she'd met briefly the other night were all on the rolling platform, throwing red and green beaded necklaces at the crowd along with candy canes and chocolate kisses. But the big hit had nothing to do with the free offerings and everything to do with the animal carrying the sacks the women were drawing from. One very live reindeer donned a red nose. How those happy ladies got the animal to keep it on she had no idea but somehow it worked.

"More hot chocolate, dear?" Fiona Hart held out a thermos.

"No thank you. If I drink any more I'm going to float home."

Even Mrs. Hart's chuckle was ever so ladylike. Kelly wouldn't mind a chance at an entire photo shoot with this woman. She had a classic elegance about her that shone through whether she was wearing an exotic kaftan or bundled in a woolen hat and scarf set.

Kelly's phone buzzed with a text and she opted to ignore it. Whatever it was she couldn't be bothered with it. Then a small pang of guilt struck. What if her mom was in trouble? Or her cousin? Or worse, one of her cousin's kids. Not that there was much Kelly could do from all the way up North.

Another buzz sounded and she slid the phone out of her pocket. Her boss. Now she was positive she didn't want to take the call. Not that her editor was a horror, Kelly simply didn't want to deal with the real world. Not now, not yet. She turned the phone to silent, no vibrate, no buzzing. She was not going to let her boss leech into this lovely evening.

"Look what we have here." Lily came hurrying up to the row of chairs in the corded off area in front of the hardware store. "Fresh out of the oven."

From where she sat, Kelly could easily recognize the tantalizing aroma of blueberry muffins.

"I wanted to make cranberry. You know, Christmas and all, but apparently there's a local cranberry shortage." Lily shrugged and waved her hands in the air in a familiar gesture of surrender, or perhaps incredulity.

"And why," Mrs. Hart smiled ever so slightly at her granddaughter, "are you baking at this late hour on parade night?"

"We got slammed with last minute orders for all the after parties. Figured as long as we had to stay late to bake, might as well make something warm and fun for us."

"I, for one," Iris broke open a steaming muffin, "am not complaining at all. Thank you."

Cindy popped a morsel into her mouth and groaned. "Oh how I miss your late night baking extravaganzas."

It made sense that once upon a time when all the girls lived under one roof, there might have been plenty of late night bakefests. Now that they were all in separate homes, warm from the oven muffins must be as much of a treat for the sisters as it was for Kelly.

Once the parade drew to a close, the crowds lingered, talking, laughing, and some folks were happy to return to their holiday shopping. Many of the stores had remained open, the clerks in the doorways watching the parade pass by. Not a single soul on Main Street displayed even a tinge of the humbug attitude.

"We'd better hurry." Fiona popped up from her seat. "Floyd and his cronies, and the Merry Widows and their contingency are coming to Hart House for dessert."

"I made sure everything was all set up before we left." Lucy folded her chair and stacked it along the lamppost with the others before turning to face

Glenn. "You two should take a minute and drive by the church. The manger is lit and live starting tonight. It's worth the detour."

As anxious as Kelly was to get home and run through the photos she'd taken, not to mention taste her way through all the goodies served, she was even more intrigued to see the manger she'd contributed to come to life. The thought almost made her laugh. She'd had more part in contributing and building things this past week than she'd had in the last who knew how many years.

"You up for it?" Keeping his gaze on Kelly, Glenn stacked his folding chair with the others.

Kelly nodded. "Absolutely." She gathered her belongings, helped stack a few more folded chairs, and in a flash, no one would ever have known the streets only minutes before had been filled with bystanders watching a parade.

"I've been looking forward to this." Glenn slid into the passenger side of Kelly's car. "Really glad you wanted to drive by."

"I've been looking forward to it too. Since my grandparents died I've never really been a part of holiday traditions."

"Good memories?"

"The best." Her heart lifted as the visions of her childhood days spent with her grandparents played in the back of her head. "In a different way, my grandmother reminds me of Mrs. Hart. Not quite as elegant, but just as comforting. She loved to bake and decorate and wrap gifts. Oh how she loved wrapping gifts. Every so often the floor under the tree would be overflowing with gifts and then we'd realize she'd been wrapping things for the neighbors, or her friends. Sometimes she'd keep them safe at her house until Christmas Eve when her friends would come get them. It gave her so much joy. I think in some small way she felt as though she was also giving the gift."

"My grandmother always said it's the little things that make living worthwhile. Sounds like your grandmother may have thought the same way."

"Definitely. Probably why it takes me almost as long to pick out the wrapping paper and ribbon as it took to find the gift in the first place."

"Actually, if you think about it, in many ways your photos are small gifts to the world. I'd say there's even more of your grandmother in you than you realized."

Though Glenn's conclusions might have been a bit of a stretch, it still made her feel good to think that even a little part of her grandmother was still with her. She was still smiling at the thought when she turned the corner and the church manger came into view. "Oh my."

"It does make an impression, doesn't it?" Glenn didn't say anything else. He really didn't have to. They had been expecting to see the volunteers from the congregation taking turns posing in the manger, but the live animals had caught Kelly off guard. Not so much the sheep, or the donkey her boss had mentioned, but what really had her stunned at first sight was the full grown camel. Though the animals alone weren't the startling part of the scene, the serenity and peace coming from the scene made her step on the brakes and just look. Absorb. As much as she wanted to get back to Hart House, she hated to step on the gas and keep rolling down the street. She wanted to stay and soak in the love of the season permeating every square inch of space in this lovely old town, but she had a job to do and there was no putting it off.

While the Hart home filled with friends and family, all eager to nosh on the delectable goodies that had been prepared for the evening, Kelly loaded the shots she'd taken from her camera to her laptop. Knowing that her editor was most likely calling to press her about the photos for the holiday spread, with the General's permission, she slipped away to his office to do the job she'd actually been sent here for. Notepad at her side for old fashioned backup, she moved copies of the keeper photos to a different folder.

"Oh, now what have we here?" Katie O'Leary, the dear family friend with just enough of an Irish accent to make a person's mind wander to green pastures and dreams of leprechauns and pots of gold, had quietly entered the room and watched over Kelly's shoulder. "These are truly wonderful."

"Thank you." Seeing the surprise pleasure in Katie's eyes made Kelly almost giggle with delight. She'd hoped everyone would think the photos were as good as she did.

"You've done a superb job with the nativity scene. I bet Pastor Bob would like copies if you're allowed."

"I'll talk to him." Looking at one of the photos with the camel, she wondered if Katie would know more about it. "Where do you suppose they get the animals?"

"Local sanctuary. Has everything from lions and tigers to exotic birds. Most are rescues from idiots who thought they could care for them like a stray cat or parakeet." Katie's eyes remained focused on the screen as she studied each photo.

When Katie gestured at Kelly to move to the next screen, and a deep set furrow formed in Katie's brow, Kelly thought maybe the woman had changed her mind about the quality of the photographs.

After flipping through almost every screen, Katie straightened, nodded her head and finally lost the frown. "I know you make your living from this, so of course I knew you had to be good, but I failed to understand just how good you probably had to be for your job. These are amazing. And not just the way you captured the spirit of the town – but the spirit of the people."

"I had hoped."

"You did more than hope, Kelly. Go back a few screens."

Kelly clicked back through the photos until she came to the page with the one photo in particular that Katie's lips had pressed more tightly together.

"That's the one."

A candid shot of the General and his wife, sitting side by side, holding hands. Kelly had snapped the shot just as the two had turned their attention from the tree lighting to each other. At the time Kelly had been impressed with how when one looked at the other, immediately he or she turned and met glances. The inner connection was startling, and this time Kelly caught it on film, so to speak, and had been truly delighted with the result. A second later, she'd caught Poppy at her grandmother's side and a moment later, all the granddaughters had gathered behind the patriarch and his wife. Kelly had snapped a few candids before asking the family to pose. She'd been thinking of having it blown up and framed as a Christmas gift.

"Yes, tis a gift you have. The General and Fiona will be delighted."

"Delighted?"

"When they unwrap your gift."

"My gift?" Was this woman reading her mind?

"Surely, it's occurred to you that this is too good a moment in time to leave trapped in a file somewhere in cyberspace."

Ah, she was merely presuming. Kelly studied this woman, who at more than one gathering had been described to her as the soul of the town by some and an angel by others. She actually wondered if there was more to the comment than people realized. "I was actually just thinking that."

Katie's eyes shined with a knowing twinkle and Kelly decided, just in case, she'd only think nice thoughts around this woman.

"Sometimes taking a stroll through the woods is better than keeping to the footpath."

"I beg your pardon?" Or maybe she wasn't an angel, she was simply a little crazy.

Katie patted her reassuringly on the shoulder. "Just remembering something my sainted grandmother used to say from time to time when stumbling across a person with talent. I'd best be getting back to the party and let you finish your work so you can join us."

As quickly and quietly as Katie had appeared, she'd disappeared from view.

Turning her attention back to the family portrait, Kelly studied the shot. She was quite proud of how it had turned out. It had taken a little bit to make the dim lighting work in her favor, but she'd been quite pleased. Now she stared at the picture and wondered how could any rational person's mind go from a family in holiday lights to walking in the woods? Shaking her head, Kelly hit send on the email with the chosen photos to her boss and pushed to her feet, muttering, "The woman's probably just a little crazy."

CHAPTER TEN

As amazing as the sunsets were on the West Coast, and Glenn did love them, the draw of the morning sun over the lake was something he was going to miss when it was time to go home. There were a lot of things he was going to miss and he didn't quite know what to do about it. Rather than continue to toss and turn, he opted for climbing out of bed a little earlier than usual and taking a nice walk along the water.

"You're up awfully early." The soft familiar voice surprised him.

"Pot calling the kettle black?"

Her head tipped slightly back, a soft rumble of laughter escaped. "My grandmother used to say *donkey calling the piggy big ears.* Mind if I join you?"

"Please do." He took a chance extending his hand in Kelly's direction, delighted when she slipped her fingers in his.

"Something in particular have you up this early?"

"Nothing in particular." He kicked a small rock to the side of the path. "This trip is going by much faster than I anticipated. Pretty soon it's going to be time to head back home, back to work. What about you?"

"I guess a little of the same. I've been dreading returning to the land of great cell phone communication and Internet connections. This whole being unplugged thing is something I think I could get used to."

His gaze on the stony path following the water's edge, it struck him how absolutely perfect everything about this moment was. The morning air, crisp but not really cold. The only sounds the rustling of dry leaves in the wind. The lake for as far as the eye could see lay pristine under a blanket of snow. Hints of golden tones shining above the treed skyline in the distance. The warm hand of the woman he couldn't stop thinking about firmly in his. Everything about the start of the day was perfect, except maybe one. Slowing his steps, he blew out a soft breath, gathering up his courage. "Have you ever found yourself coming up against something that you really thought you would want, but hadn't thought you could ever have?"

"I think everyone feels that way at some point in their life. Women probably more so. We're still conditioned to want the elusive Prince Charming and the happily ever after that comes with a castle and cute little princes and princesses running about. Except reality and expectations don't always line up. Nowhere in the fairy tale is there the mention of careers, bills, deadlines, or deadbeat princes."

"Princes aren't the only ones who disappoint." He glanced off into the distance, expecting the pangs of pain and regret to strike as they always did whenever anyone reminded him of his failed marriage, but nothing happened. "I can't say that the whole fairytale thing was a big part of my childhood, but I can certainly understand reality and expectations colliding."

"Mom said women's lib short changed the female gender. A popular TV commercial when she was a little girl bragged how a modern woman could bring home the bacon then fry it up in a pan. Seemed unfair that before the women's lib movement all men had to do was bring home the bacon and all women had to do was fry it up. Then one day women had the privilege of doing both."

"So what do you want that you can't have?"

"Honestly, until recently I pretty much thought with a lot of work, I could have anything I wanted."

"Until recently?"

Stopping, she bent down and weighing a small stone in her hand, straightened. Taking aim, she sent the stone skipping across the water. "This assignment has me rethinking what I really want."

"And what do you think you might really want?" More right now than even five minutes ago, he knew exactly what he wanted.

Still standing in place, she turned to face him. "Less busy, more life."

He wasn't sure what to say to that.

"Despite the grind of daily life, the people here seem to do a lot more living in their small town with friends and family than I have done jet setting across the continents. I've been to the most beautiful and romantic places in the world. Paris. Rome. Venice. And yet," her gaze locked with his, "none of those places seem to be able to compete with this place in all its winter glory."

Whether she had meant to look so absolutely kissable in the morning light or not, he simply could not resist the temptation any longer. Shifting to stand fully in front of her, he let his free hand lift up and cradle the side of her face. Hesitating a fraction of a second, he saw her eyes widen with surprise as his mouth gently pressed against hers.

The kiss was soft and delicate, and he forced himself to draw back long before he wanted to or he might never want to let go. Not moving, he watched her face as her eyelids slowly lifted.

The surprise he'd seen a moment ago was gone, and a glimmer of something he couldn't make out shone back at him and a lazy smile slowly appeared. "Can we do that again?"

A satisfied grin tugged at the corners of his lips. "Absolutely." This time he dared to pull her closer against him. His arms looping around her, he almost lost his breath when her fingers curled into the back of his neck. Beyond any doubt, this was a woman he could kiss for the rest of his life. Right here. On this spot. Forever. Once again, gathering his wits, he eased back and sucking in a deep breath, resisted the urge to once more press his lips against hers, and instead settled for a chaste kiss on her forehead. His lips lingering longer than they should have, he mumbled against her soft skin, "I've been wanting to do that for days."

She leaned into him, her head resting on his shoulder. "Why didn't you?"

"Too many people everywhere all the time." He brushed his fingers through her hair. "I didn't think you'd appreciate it in front of everyone. Especially Lucy."

"Now I almost wish she'd locked us in a closet."

"I thought it was a shed?" He could stand like this for days. Maybe years.

She didn't move. "I think it might have been both."

Glenn chuckled softly. "If Lucy hadn't been in the room to confirm some of the wild stories we heard, I'd have thought people were pulling our leg."

"I know." She remained rooted in place.

"As much as it pains me to say this." His hands dropped to his sides.

Kelly blew out a sigh, took a step in retreat, and looked up at him. "Long day coming."

He nodded. "The pastor will be expecting you at the church first thing after breakfast."

"Remind me why I agreed to do holiday family portraits for any of the parishioners who wanted one?"

"Because Katie made sure half the town including the pastor knew what a master you were at things other than high fashion and Christmas trees, and you volunteered."

"That must have been the wine talking."

"You'd only had one glass." He tugged at her hand to turn her back toward Hart Land. "Face it. You're a nice person." Not a shadow of a dark side had appeared and his nice girl radar had given up on sending him warning signals. He was just too darn happy to care about where this, whatever this was, could go.

"I'm telling you," her grin widened, "there's something special about this town."

Didn't he know that. A gust of cold wind kicked up from the water and he instinctively drew her closer, draping his arm around her shoulders.

"Thanks." She leaned into his side. "Is it me or did the temperatures just drop like a million degrees?"

"Maybe half a million. I heard someone last night say that there's a nasty storm forecasted to blow in tonight."

"I'm not sure it's going to wait that long."

The sky above seemed clear and pleasant, but what was the old saying: red sky in morning, sailor take warning. Whoever it was that pointed out the weather forecast was rarely reliable looked to be in for a nasty surprise. On the other hand, thoughts of a warm fireplace and Kelly at his side wasn't a bad idea at all.

"So, what prompted your question?"

A blank expression crossed Glenn's face.

"Something you really thought you wanted but didn't think you could ever have?"

"I did ask that, didn't I?" A lazy smile tipped one corner of his mouth upward.

"You did."

"I suppose, like you, this town is having a bit of an affect on me. All the happy people. Happy couples. The merriment, joy, and sheer delight in the season. A delight that I suspect is probably alive and well in the middle of summer as much as the middle of the holiday season."

"It does feel that way doesn't it?"

"It does. And it's making me face things about the way I live my life."

She swallowed a chuckle. Was it just them, or did Hart Land have this affect on everyone?

"Not only am I rethinking what makes a home, I'm thinking maybe it's time I did more than just unpack my bags. I can't let what Amanda did drive my actions for the rest of my life."

To Kelly's chagrin, the best reception for cell phones and wi-fi at the lake was along the beach. They'd barely set foot by the sandy edge of the path when her phone rang, cutting Glenn off. Frankly, she was surprised she hadn't heard sooner from her boss. She probably should have followed up on the photos she'd sent the other night, but she just hadn't felt like it. She'd wanted to preserve whatever magical bubble she'd walked into, but there was no point in putting it off. This morning's suspension of reality had been shattered by the dumb phone. "Hello."

"It's about time you answered the phone."

"You know we have lousy reception up here."

"That's why I've been texting you for days!" Her editor was not using her inside voice.

Kelly tapped at the phone. No backed up messages. Or logs of calls. "I don't see any messages on my phone."

"I used the emergency number. What good is an emergency number if no one responds?"

"You texted the emergency contact number I gave you?"

"Of course I did. I needed you back in New York two days ago."

"Caroline, that's a land line."

"Land line? Who the hell still has a landline?"

"The Harts. That's why I gave it to you. The only sure way to reach me if it was important." Still walking, she knew if she didn't stop she'd lose signal pretty soon, but the words her editor had shouted finally registered. Key words being *New York* and *days ago*.

"If you hadn't picked up I was going to have to break down and send Jimmy Olsen to photograph the biggest scoop we've had in a decade."

Able to hear the entire conversation, Glenn's brow wrinkled with confusion.

Kelly hit mute and softly explained. "She always calls the probational photographers Jimmy Olsen."

"Got it," Glenn whispered back.

"How fast can you get here?" Caroline asked.

"I can't." Not only had she committed to the photographs of the parishioners, the church was counting on her for the pageant photos as well. Besides, she didn't want to be the go-to photographer because she didn't have family over the holidays.

"Of course you can. If you hurry you can beat the storm before it hits."

"You know we're expecting a storm?"

"You really are out of touch. The whole East Coast is expecting to be slammed with more snow than the North Pole. There's already two inches in Philly. It's moving faster than expected, so you've got to boogie."

"I told you I can't."

Dead silence greeted her for longer than she'd expected. Not a good sign.

"You know how it works. We need you, you go. It's why you're one of our best and get the plum assignments."

A couple of weeks ago she would have argued that Podunk New England was not a plum assignment, but right now, there wasn't any place else she wanted to be. "I can't."

"If you want a job when you get home, you may want to rethink that. I'll expect you at my desk in a few hours."

Whether Caroline hung up or the connection was lost, Kelly wasn't sure.

"That doesn't sound good." That deep-set line between Glenn's brow had returned.

"No." She stared at the blank screen trying to remember if she'd ever been threatened with loss of her job before. Not a single instance came to mind of being threatened or of her saying no to an assignment. She had no idea how serious Caroline was and she wasn't completely sure how she felt about that.

"So now what?"

"Now," she straightened her shoulders, "we join the family for breakfast and then I'll head to the church to take photos as promised."

"You sure? The pastor and parishioners will understand that your paying job needs you."

"I'm sure they would, but I'm tired of asking

how high every time she says jump because someone else failed her, or being given an assignment during a holiday simply because I don't have a family of my own. I gave my word to the folks in this town and I intend to keep it. If I don't have a job when the season is over, well, my camera and I will just have to figure something else out."

A slow, sure smile took over Glenn's face and Kelly drew on all her self discipline to keep from leaning in and kissing that grin off his face. She wasn't ready to tell him just yet that for all the good reasons she could muster to let go of her job, there was only one good reason for wanting to stay longer, and it wasn't the magic of Lawford. The man silently at her side, showing support, and making her heart dance, with one real kiss had completely shifted her world.

The sun had fully risen but did little to warm the day. Neither stopped at their cabins, but hurried up the hill to meet the Harts for breakfast. On the front porch, Kelly stomped the snow from her boots and opened the front door. As expected, any morning activity came from the direction of the kitchen.

Gloves in pocket, Kelly slid on to the nearest island stool and blew into her hands. "I really think this time the weather forecasters may have gotten it right. It is freezing out there."

A cup of coffee slid in front of her. Glenn stood at her side. "This should help warm you up. Milk and no sugar, right?"

She nodded and wrapped her hands around the warm mug. "Thank you." Was it absolutely ridiculous that she was thrilled almost to the point of giddy laughter because he'd made her a cup of coffee. Not just any cup of coffee, a cup with milk and no sugar. He'd remembered how she likes her coffee. And on top of that, he'd poured her a cup before making his own. When it came down to what really mattered in life, things couldn't get any better.

Across the island, Lucy had casually glanced in their direction. She hadn't said anything, but Kelly caught the woman grinning at them. Was it that obvious that her stomach was in a state of perpetual butterflies in flight every time Glenn stood in the same room as her?

The sound of stomping feet at the backdoor had Kelly looking up.

"It's started snowing. I think this is the beginning." Poppy pulled a knit cap from her head, shoved it in her coat pocket, then hung the coat on a nearby hook. "Thought I'd check if you've got anything you need me to do for you this morning."

"That and you heard Lucy's making her French toast casserole for breakfast, didn't you?" Fiona grinned at her youngest granddaughter.

"Busted." Poppy laughed and crossed the room to peek into the oven.

"Not yet." Lucy gently tapped at Poppy, shooing her away.

Poppy flashed a short pout. "Party pooper."

"As long as you're here," Lucy waved at Poppy, "might as well help set the table."

"Have we been here long enough to help?" Kelly stood in place, waiting for the go ahead.

"I suppose." Lucy let out a sigh. "You can help set the table."

"I'll get the dishes." Glenn pushed away from the island and without direction, went straight to the cabinet with all the plates.

Gathering the silverware from the nearby drawer, Kelly watched Glenn collecting enough dishes for the entire family. A long time ago there had been a cartoon circulating that claimed there was nothing sexier than a man cleaning house. At the time she'd thought it was the dumbest thing she'd ever read. Until now. The way her heart fluttered at the sight of Glenn carrying dishes into the dining room, Kelly was in big trouble. Walking away from this man and this place might very well break her fluttering heart. And what the heck was she going to do about that?

CHAPTER ELEVEN

"Looks like Mother Nature is putting on a show of her own." Kelly glanced away from the window. "I hope this won't affect your grandparents' flight tomorrow."

"If I know anything about my grandfather, he won't let a little winter storm stop his plans. Even if they have to walk to the lake, they'll be here tomorrow night." Glenn and his brother had spent a long while last night revisiting the scattered memories with their grandfather. For the first time in a long time, for a lot of reasons, he was very much looking forward to this family holiday.

"Good. I'm excited to meet your grandparents."

All through breakfast Glenn had kept his eye on Kelly. Most people would have been upset or anxious after the ultimatum her boss had tossed out. He didn't like the idea of the threat of losing her job hanging over her head. Especially this time of year. So far there wasn't even the slightest sign of her even thinking about her career.

The only thing she'd focused on was getting to the church to start taking the parishioners portraits, but now that Glenn had taken a few moments to look away from her and out the window, he wondered if that was a good idea.

"Oh my." Kelly's eyes rounded at the wall of white flakes falling outside.

"It is coming down a bit." At the near top of a

six foot ladder, Fiona Hart slid a sprig of mistletoe onto a hook and climbed down. "Better take the Jeep. It has snow tires and is higher off the ground than your car. Sometimes these storms can dump several inches in a flash."

In two quick strides, Glenn stepped up beside Mrs. Hart before she could finish folding the ladder and carry it off. "Let me help."

Shaking her head, the woman who always looked ready to grace the cover of a magazine, even now when she clearly intended to lug a ladder about the house, she looked so well dressed. "I do this every year. The exercise is good for me."

Glenn had no idea how old she was, but somehow climbing up and down a ladder struck him as more dangerous than exercise. For anyone. "I really don't mind."

"No." She shook her head again. "You two go on to the church. There's a big day ahead of us."

As if barking his agreement, Wooster let out two short woofs.

"I think he wants to go with you." Lucy closed the dishwasher door with a hip bump. "I'm sure the pastor won't mind. Poppy used to take their dog to work every day before they officially adopted him."

Fiona had moved the ladder to the opposite side of the kitchen, and as she'd done before, climbed up, hooked the sprig of mistletoe on a hook over the back door, and climbed down. "Just in case the storm gets worse before it loses steam, remember to wait it out at Mabel's. They'll have lots of pie and hot coffee to keep you happy until it's safe to drive home."

None of the precautions delivered with nonchalance by the household did anything to reassure him. This much snow was just a bit much for this California boy.

"I'm ready if you are?" Camera bag in hand, Kelly looked as eager as a little kid on Christmas morning.

His gaze drifted over to the window. The snow still seemed to be falling in cascades and yet he was the only one with any concerns. Clearly he needed to spend more time in states with white winters. And now was as good a time as any to make friends with the snow. "Let's go."

They were almost out of the kitchen when Lucy called out for them to wait and ran around the island waving a small brown paper bag in her hand. "I almost forgot. Made some of those energy muffins that Lily bakes for her husband."

"Cole is a bit of a health aficionado." Fiona smiled to no one in particular. "Of course, he has to be. Wouldn't do to have a fireman run out of steam halfway up the stairs in a burning building."

"No." Glenn agreed. "Not a good thing at all." He accepted Lucy's offering and when a toothy grin took over her face, and her eyes lifted to the archway above them, he realized they'd been had. Lucy had called at just the right moment to catch them under the newly hung mistletoe.

"Tradition, you know." Lucy continued to beam happily.

"Mustn't disappoint." Kelly grinned at him.

Ignoring the audience of two smiling at them, he leaned in for a brief peck on the lips and forced himself to take a half step in retreat. When he looked up, both Lucy and Fiona were grinning like proud mama bears. If mama bears could grin.

In the foyer, he helped Kelly into her coat, wrapped a scarf around his neck for extra insulation, and squatted down by his dog. "Are you sure you want to come?"

Wooster sat his butt down in front of Glenn,

wagged his tail across the hardwood floors, and let out one sharp woof.

"There could be a lot of snow when it's time to come home?"

Again, the small dog lifted his chin and let out a sharp bark.

"Guess we're all braving the deluge of snow."

Kelly beat him out the front door. From the porch she slapped her hands together and squealed. "I feel like a little kid." She spun around to face him. "Do you think when we get back we can take some time to make snow angels?"

Right about now if she'd asked him to dive into the frozen lake, he would. "I think that's a great idea."

Still grinning like the Cheshire Cat, Kelly skipped down the porch steps and with Wooster on her heels, hurried to the General's Jeep parked in front. Now he was the one who wished he had a camera. Everything, snow and all, was simply picture perfect. If only he could make this moment last forever.

"Good grief." Kelly hadn't expected to see so many cars lining the curb outside the church. "Do you think they're all here for portraits?"

"Could be." Glenn shrugged. "No one seems to care much about the snow."

"Probably because they get so much of it all winter long."

"That they do." He pulled into an available space in the church lot and they hurried inside where several families waited in the sanctuary. Moms corralled their little ones, dads fussed with their ties, and Pastor Bob hurried in their direction.

"So glad you're here. I have to run to the hospital, but didn't want to leave with all these people waiting for their photo session."

"Hospital?" Kelly did little to hide the alarm in her voice.

"It's Nancy. She tripped coming up the front steps. Landed hard on her arm. Her wrist actually. Poppy was kind enough to drive her over despite her objections, but now she's refusing treatment, insisting she needs to play the piano for the pageant and can't do it with her wrist in a cast."

"Oh, no." Kelly glanced in the direction of the entrance to the main hall. "Does the church have someone who backs her up normally if there's an occasion when she can't play?"

The pastor shook his head. "I suspect that's why Nancy is in such a hurry to get back."

Her gaze lifted to meet Glenn's.

He smiled and squeezed her hand. "I may be able to help."

"Do you play?" the pastor asked.

Glenn bit back a smile. "A little."

The pastor shoved his hand out and slapped him on the shoulder. "Then you're elected. I'll tell Nancy so she stops fretting. The iPad with all the music is on the piano if you want to get in a little practice before the kids show up for a pre-show run through."

"I'll go look as soon as I help Kelly set up."

"Sounds like a plan. Gotta run." The pastor trotted past them and out the large wooden doors.

To his surprise, entire families of parishioners continued to brave the snowfall to have their portraits done. Apparently he really was too much of a Californian and had let the predictions for bad weather spook him unnecessarily. To locals, a little, or even a lot, of snow was as normal as a sunny day in Southern California.

Hovering around lunchtime, the crowd of parishioners slowed to a trickle and full stop at about the same time Pastor Bob came hurrying through the door with Poppy in tow.

"Well, that was easier said than done." Poppy shrugged out of her coat. "I never realized how stubborn Nancy could be."

"Not necessarily a bad thing." The pastor hung his coat and hat beside Poppy's. "It's one of the many qualities that makes her so dependable. My predecessor had her name on the top of the list of go-to people for whenever we needed anything at the church. He wasn't wrong."

Kelly glanced in the direction of the church doors. "Does that mean she's going to play with a broken wrist?"

"Not a chance." A smile took over Poppy's face. "We left her at Hart house with my grandmother and Lucy."

Glenn couldn't help the burst of laughter that escaped from deep in his gut. "Oh, you guys play dirty. No way that sweet old lady can escape the watch of both Fiona and Lucy to come play in her condition."

"Somebody had to do it." The pastor shrugged and turned to Glenn. "Have you had a chance to look at the music?"

"I'm afraid he's been helping me." Kelly grimaced.

The pastor nodded. "I see. If you think it's too much for you, we have some free recorded music we could use for some of the performance, and do without a few other parts. I'm sure all the parents and guests will be perfectly delighted without the live piano performance."

"I'm sure it'll be fine. This time of year, there's

always a high demand for holiday music."

"Oh good. I guess I never asked." Pastor Bob dropped his keys on a nearby desk. "Do you play for your church?"

"Not really." Glenn didn't want to mention until now that he hadn't set foot in a church since his wedding day.

Kelly looped her hand through Glenn's elbow and beamed up at the pastor. "The Peterson's are a talented family. He plays the piano for a living."

"Oh." A pleasant look of surprise crossed the pastor's face. "In a band?"

"You could say that." Glenn smiled.

"A band?" Incredulity dripped from Poppy's words. "I don't know that I would call the Southern California Symphony Orchestra a band."

"Orchestra?" Kelly and the pastor echoed with bookended expressions of astonishment.

"You didn't say anything about a symphony." Kelly took a step back, her brows dipping into a perfect V, and Glenn realized that the one time she'd asked about what he did, they'd been interrupted before he'd gotten a chance to correct her assumption that when he said he played the piano for a living, that he was a lounge lizard. Somehow they never came back to the subject and it never occurred to him to bring it up again.

"I never got the chance. Does it matter that much what I do?" His heart was nearly in his throat. Everything had gone so well with Kelly, if he'd screwed everything up over a simple miscommunication and hurt feelings, he would never forgive himself.

Her brows remained creased for another long minute before her expression relaxed. There was still disappointment in her eyes, but not the flash of anger he thought he'd detected a moment ago. "I suppose it doesn't."

"Well." Poppy cleared her throat. "I have work to do before the pageant tonight."

"Me too," the pastor muttered. Both he and Poppy scurried away from the entry into their offices, closing the doors that he'd not once seen shut before.

He closed the small gap she'd put between them and took Kelly's hands between his, then lowered his voice. Last chance to plead his case. "I wasn't trying to hide anything from you. I honestly forgot to bring it up again after we were interrupted that afternoon when you asked me about my job."

For a second he thought his words might fall on deaf ears, then she blew out a small sigh, nodded, and the light returned to her gaze. "That was the conversation where the three dogs came galloping into the room, with Wooster landing on your lap and the General laughing from the doorway."

"That would be the one." Already his heart felt lighter. Happier.

"The conversation turned to West Point and the General's days with your grandfather."

Glenn dared to smile at her. "And how they'd all come together to bring Alan and Cindy together."

Her smile widened. "I guess I did jump to the conclusion you played in a club of some kind, didn't I?"

"Natural assumption. There are way more piano players in bars and lounges than in symphony orchestras. Forgive me?"

"Nothing to forgive." She stretched up onto her tippy toes and gave him a slight peck on the lips. "But seriously, do you need to practice or something?"

He laughed. "I should look at the program, but without the kids to test the timing on, I'll just have to wing it tonight."

"Wing it?" She sucked in a deep breath and blew it out slowly. "I feel like there's been a lot of that going on lately."

"And look how well it's working out."

Pulling Kelly in for more than a peck on the lips, the church doors blew open with a crack and Cole, Lily's husband, and another fireman came through the doors. "You guys may be the only ones in town with lights."

"And heat," the other guy added.

"What's going on?" Pastor Bob and Poppy appeared in the hall.

"The storm took out a transformer on the other side of the mountain," Cole answered. "It's created a domino affect halfway to Boston and with the bigger part of the storm yet to come, there's no ETA on when power will be restored."

The other guy shook his head. "We're all doing door to door checks to see who might not be prepared to hang on for the night. So far you're the only ones with lights."

Pastor Bob nodded. "With the extra money from the fire fund we had one of those new automatic generators connected to the gas line. It's supposed to kick in as soon as there's a power loss."

"We have one of those at Hart House," Poppy chimed in. "Well, the main house anyhow."

"Better send anyone who isn't prepared here," the pastor suggested. "Could be a good way to ensure a standing room only crowd for the pageant."

Both firemen chuckled. "Will do. We've got to run. Let us know if you hear of anyone in trouble."

"Looks like it's going to be a long night." The pastor turned on his heel. "I'd better start calling our list of elderly parishioners."

"Need any help?" Glenn asked.

The pastor shook his head. "Poppy and I can cover it. You go ahead and do whatever you need to for tonight."

"Done." Glenn reached for Kelly's hand and tugged her beside him. "Guess you get to watch me tickle the ivories."

She leaned into him and chuckled. "Best offer I've had all day."

CHAPTER TWELVE

"I don't suppose you had anything to do with this?" Fiona Hart stood at the second floor linen closet pulling out fresh sheets for the empty rooms that she expected to fill up with folks unprepared for the night and needing shelter.

"Me?" Lucy gathered blankets from a different closet. "Do with what?"

"The power outage."

"You think I had something to do with that?"

Fiona stopped, her hand on a top shelf. When Lucy put it that way, it did sound rather ridiculous. The woman had done so many strange things in her day in an effort to bring people together Fiona couldn't help but wonder. "Never mind. It was a silly question. I'm just worried about the older folks on the mountain without heat or electricity."

"Every fire department on the mountain is out making sure everyone is okay. They are checking all the wood-burning stoves and fireplaces to make sure there were no fire hazards and notifying Jake and a few others if somebody needs a wood delivery. This isn't the first blizzard this mountain has lived through."

"And it won't be the last."

"Between us and the Hilltop Inn, there'll be plenty of safe haven for anyone who needs it."

"One of the blessings of an Inn as old as Hilltop – every room with a working fireplace and keeping the old wood burning stove for decoration, but making sure it could still be used in an emergency."

"Yep. We've got it all covered. By morning it will all be cleared up and everyone will have had a nice cozy night with friends and family."

Arms laden with linens, Fiona cast a sideway glance at Lucy. Something about calling a blizzard-driven night of chaos cozy had her mind asking stupid questions again. She really had to stop letting her imagination run away with her.

The church hall had been filling up since as early as word had gotten out that the church had heat and electricity and the evening performance was not canceled. Kelly had barely gotten the chance to hear Glenn play a song or two before the people had begun to arrive.

Anybody with common sense knew that in order to play an instrument in a highly acclaimed symphony orchestra, that person had to be good. Talent had to be off the charts. Yet, not till she saw the gentle way those long thin fingers caressed the keys, and the amazing sounds that came from the piano, did concept and reality meet.

She'd been sitting beside Cindy and the rest of the Hart family waiting for the pageant to begin.

Fiona Hart leaned into her from the other side. "Louise told me that there are quite a few families who are braving the blizzard conditions solely to hear Glenn perform."

"You're kidding?"

The lovely woman shook her head. "Once a few key folks realized exactly who Glenn is, the word spread like fire on gas soaked kindling. This is going to be quite the treat."

Pride bloomed deep inside her. Anyone would think he was more than just a friend. After such a short amount of time, some would argue they weren't truly friends, but merely acquaintances. Yet, the joy bursting inside her when Glenn stood beside the piano and bowed to the loudly applauding crowd had nothing to do with the sentiments of mere acquaintances. Magic or not, she was in full blown, head over heels love with Glenn Peterson.

"Here they come." Fiona rubbed her hands together and the crowd settled down for the beginning of the pageant. From the first appearance of Mary and Joseph on stage, to the multitude of winged angels, and even the parading across the stage of the clomping camel, the story was sweet, and moving, and so very well done.

When the production was over, the audience stood and applauded for so long the pastor finally had to take center stage and ask everyone to be seated. He gave thanks to the kids who had practiced tirelessly, the people who had contributed their time and skill with sets and costumes, and of course thanked Glenn for stepping in at the last minute. "I would also like to share that the fire department has informed me that with the help of extra volunteers, every single resident of Lawford has been accounted for and is either in excellent shape for the next day or so or has been transported to one of the local safe havens. We have a wonderful community we can be proud of."

It took a few more minutes for everyone to stop applauding and chattering and for the pastor to get their attention again. "I'd like to add we have food and drink in the vestibule thanks to the contributions from our beloved Katie O'Leary, and of course Lily, as well as Mabel's diner. Everyone, please enjoy!"

Everything on the tables was irresistibly delicious. A round powder covered cookie in hand, she was about to take a bite when a warm breath touched her neck.

"Is that as good as it looks?" Glenn was looking at the cookie, but somehow she didn't think that's what he was referring to. He grabbed hold of her hand and urged her to follow him.

Despite the enormous crowd packed into every nook of the church facility, he still managed to find one quiet corner for just the two of them.

"You were fantastic."

"Those kids were fantastic. Seeing them all backstage getting ready, the excitement, the crying, the nerves, but in the end each and every one of them was so proud and happy to be up there on stage, whether they had lines or just a place to stand. It was really something to watch."

"I really do think there's something almost magical about this place."

"I've avoided a lot of things the last few years, and didn't even realize it. Friends, family," he waved one hand around him, "church. I let one single focused woman taint my views on life and love."

"I don't know what to say. I'm sorry that your ex hurt you, but I can't lie, I'm glad you're here now."

"Funny how we convince ourselves that all is well. That the past is not dictating our present. I mean, I'm not dumb enough to think that many of my choices were because of what Amanda did, but I guess I was a little too blind to see that my world didn't have to be built on the past. Amanda was smart, beautiful, very wealthy, and I didn't care about any of it. She was also sweet and caring and loving, or at least that's what I thought, before a darker more calculated side began to surface. It turned out that being married to a musician in a symphony orchestra was somewhat of a feather in her cap. Or the family cap. But when I refused to leave my smaller community orchestra to join a more famous, or reputable, or whatever you want to call it, East Coast orchestra slot that came with longer hours, longer schedules, and all the big donor dog and pony show trappings that would be required of me and that she loved, her love and caring for me waned. Eventually everything fell apart." He actually heard himself chuckle at the memory. Something that never would have happened even a few weeks ago. "It was like the script in a really predictable and bad movie. I came home a day early from a performance out of town. She was sound asleep in the bed looking all lovely and alluring, and the conductor of the most prestigious symphony on the east coast, the one she wanted me to play in, stood naked in my bathroom, brushing his teeth."

Kelly's eyes narrowed and she hissed in a slow breath.

"Yeah. That about covers it."

"I can't even imagine."

"For years I've sworn I'm fine. I'm over it. That my family is over-reacting. That it's perfectly normal for a man to consider love and long-term relationships highly over-rated. Never bothered to connect that maybe I was closing myself off to more than just turning a condo into a home."

"Being potentially unemployed is an awful lot easier to deal with than a betrayal like that. I have an overwhelming urge to scratch the woman's eyes out."

"Thanks." Despite all the hurt, he'd never wanted to see any harm come to Amanda, he even hoped someday she found the right man for her life and aspirations, but it still made his chest swell that Kelly would want to defend him.

Her grin widened and her gaze brightened. "That's what friends are for."

Friends. And just like a pin prick to a balloon, with one word, he'd gone from delighted to deflated in a single heart beat.

"I see an all night card game in our immediate future." Cindy leaned against Kelly and chuckled. "I remember the last time a blizzard took out the power lines across the state. The card games lasted days."

"That's not completely accurate." Lily came to stand beside Glenn. "During the day, the games would break up long enough for folks to make a food run or take a nap. Then after dinner the games would resume until the next morning."

"And it went on for three days," Cindy repeated.

Kelly and Glenn and Alan turned their heads to face Lily.

"Well." Lily smiled. "Yes, I suppose if you look at it that way."

"And what may I ask are we bickering about?" Callie came over to the food table and pilfered a sampling of cookies.

"How long the card games went on for the last time we had a major power outage."

Cookie midway to her mouth, Callie froze, her mouth dropping slightly open. "Must've been a hundred years ago?"

Both Lily and Cindy nodded.

"And you expect me to remember? All night card games might not be the norm around here anymore, but they're certainly not rare either."

"She has a point." Lily waved her thumb over her shoulder at her sister.

"I see an awful lot of serious faces." Iris reached for a cookie and grinned. "Did someone confuse the salt and the sugar in the cookies?"

The teasing banter between the cousins and sisters had Kelly smiling. There was a warmth and respect that went with all the teasing and joking that made her want to stay for a lot longer than the rest of the holiday.

"It's something else, isn't it?"

She nodded. There was no need to ask what he was talking about. Everything about this assignment had turned out to be way more than she could have expected.

With a grin as large as all New England, the General came walking into the room from his office and stopped beside Glenn. "Thought you might like to know. Your grandfather caught a flight into Canada to bypass the storm. They've rented a car and expect to arrive by zero four hundred hours."

"Thank you, sir." Glenn smiled at his host.

"Do you think driving in a storm in the middle of the night is a good idea?" Kelly knew the storm was weakening as it moved north of them, but still.

Glenn shook his head. "If there's one person in this world I never worry about, it's my grandfather. If there's a problem he'll probably convince the state police to escort him. Or," he chuckled, "the snow plows."

"I see." Having met General Hart and his family, she really did have a much better understanding of the audacity and determination and quiet strength of retired military officers. She was still smiling at the General's announcement when she noticed Glenn's expression had grown more pensive. "A penny for your thoughts?"

"Honestly?"

She nodded.

"This wouldn't be a bad place to live. It's perfectly suited for family of all ages, and I don't remember ever seeing my brother happier."

Her gaze shifted to survey their surroundings. All the rooms were crowded with people. A few were snuggled into chairs or couches wrapped in blankets or sitting by the fire, but most were just enjoying themselves with no concern for the daunting situation outside. "I was thinking the same thing. Especially now that I'm fairly certain I'm unemployed."

"Did you hear from Caroline?"

Kelly shrugged. "If you mean the text that she sent hours ago telling me *last chance*, then I might have heard from her."

"No word on your job?"

She shook her head. "Jet setting is overrated anyhow."

"You really mean that?"

Her gaze bounced from one person to another in the room, landing on the General and his wife at the closest card table. "Yeah. I really do. Lily's croissants are as good, maybe better, than any I've had in France. This mountain has all the beauty of the Alps. The town can compete with any international small town. And none of those places have the heart of Hart Land."

Glenn flashed that lazy smile that made her knees weak. "Only one of the reasons I love you."

"Uh, say that again."

"That's one of the reasons?" His smile grew wider.

"The other part." She bit her lower lip and willed her heart to stop racing.

"The I love you part."

She nodded.

"I love you, Kelly Chambers, and if you're willing, I'd like to do whatever it takes to make us work. Even if it means moving to New York to play music for a big symphony orchestra."

Her heart tripped in double time. There was no way she would make him do what he didn't want to do all those years ago, but knowing she mattered enough to him for him to even suggest it made her chest fill with more emotion than she thought humanly possible. "I guess it's a good thing that I love you enough not to make you do anything so ridiculous."

The sexy smile slipped, and his eyes widened slightly. "Would you mind saying that again?"

This time she smiled. "You mean the part about not doing anything so ridiculous?"

He shook his head. "The other part."

"I love you, Glenn Peterson."

In front of God and what felt like half the town at Hart House, he pulled Kelly fully into the circle of his arms and planted a nice long kiss on her lips.

"I knew it!" Lucy's voice boomed from across the room. Carrying another tray of food, she hurried over to the table where most of the cousins had gathered. "The minute I saw Kelly hop one footed into the kitchen and the pained expression on Glenn's face, I just knew you two were meant to be together."

"You judge a couple's merit by the pain on their face?" Ralph, the old neighbor and the General's partner in card shark crime, had walked up to refill his plate. "No wonder you can't fix anyone up to last."

"That's not true. Brent, our contractor extraordinaire, and Naomi are planning their wedding."

"Ha," Ralph scoffed. "Planning and celebrating ain't the same thing."

Free of the platter, Lucy's fisted hands landed on her hips. "Well, I got these two right, didn't I?"

"What do you mean by *you*?" Ralph paused from loading his small plate to near overflowing with dessert treats.

"You don't think it was George who mixed up the luggage? Or left all the decorations in the living room with barely enough room on the sofa for two? Squished them together in the back seat of the car? Pretended the dog had eaten a pinecone so they would worry together over the dog? Face it, the togetherness was masterfully planned."

"That was all planned?" Glenn was astounded. It all seemed so natural—that is, except for the suitcase part.

Straightening her spine and grinning broadly from ear to ear, Lucy nodded. "Sure was."

"I'll be." His arm still looped around Kelly's waist, Glenn gently kissed her temple.

Standing tucked under his arm was something Kelly was looking forward to getting used to.

"See?" Lucy slapped her hands together and came short of dancing a jig. "Nothing like a little power outage to bring people together."

"Now, don't you go telling me you did that too?" Ralph shook his head and shoved a spitzbuben in his mouth.

"Not you too?" Lucy blew out a long breath and then threw her arms in the air. "Yes, it was all me. I've got the power of the almighty. Blew up a hollow tree with a couple of sticks of dynamite and sent the tree toppling onto the transformer sending the whole mountain into the dark so that Kelly and Glenn could curl up under a blanket by the fire—or by the food table—and get to really know each other."

Ralph nearly dropped the cookie. "Woman, are you insane?"

"Of course not. Where would I get my hands on dynamite?" Shaking her head and muttering 'men' Lucy stormed off.

"You know," Callie stood holding a mini cupcake in one hand, "for a minute she had me believing her."

Iris shook her head. "I certainly wouldn't put it past her."

"No." Lily shook her head rapidly from side to side. "Not even she would stoop that low."

"She *did* lock two people in a freezer," Cindy added.

Her head still moving from side to side, Lily waved her finger no. "Not the same thing as blowing up a tree and blacking out an entire mountain. No way could she have done it."

Glenn let his hand slip away from Kelly's side to catch hold of her hand and looked across the room to where Lucy could be seen smiling and laughing with Mrs. Hart. "She seems like such a sweet lady."

"She is a very sweet lady. Lily is absolutely right. Not even Lucy would stoop that low to make a match." Callie's gaze fell on Lucy working the crowd and laughing. Her brow crumpled into a frown as she turned to face her sisters. "Would she?"

EPILOGUE

"**I** do love a holiday weekend." Fiona Hart took her time wrapping the gift she'd bought. There was nothing truly artistic about gift wrapping, but she'd finally accepted that she should stick with what she did well, and she was a queen at bow making.

"I think it's going to be the best wedding gift they'll get." Lucy slathered butter on the croissant rolls and checked the oven.

"I don't know about that, but I hope they'll love it just the same."

"They will."

"Tents up and sound." The General came into the kitchen with a dog at his side.

Fiona waited for the clacking of the other dog's paws against the hardwood, but nothing. "Where's Lady?"

"She's supervising the crew with Wooster."

Fiona chuckled from deep in her belly. "Those two make quite the pair."

"What two?" Poppy came in the back door and slid heavily onto a stool.

"That would be Wooster and Lady," the General answered.

This time Poppy chuckled. "Yep. Quite the pair."

The back door opened again and Katie O'Leary came in. "What beautiful weather for a weekend wedding on the lake."

"I thought making the wedding a weekend event over Memorial Day was a brilliant idea. Since they have friends and family coming from all over the country and wanted time to spend with all of them, a three day weekend for parties was perfect."

"I'm so glad they worked out all the logistics of work and homes so far apart. I mean, I know they both had to give things up. She gave up that cushy job in New York in exchange for freelance work mostly out of Boston. And he's given up the community orchestra and is waiting out an opening with any nearby symphony." Lucy pushed the croissants into the oven. "But not only have they found a way to make Lawford Mountain their home, but now they want to marry right here too."

Arms loaded with a large white flower box, Susan, the bride's mother, followed Katie inside and directed the delivery man behind her to set the other boxes on the counter beside the crystal vases Fiona had set out earlier in the morning. "Look who I bumped into on my way back from the rehearsal."

"Ooh." Katie moved closer to the flower boxes. "I love fresh flowers."

"You're going to love these." Susan lifted the first cover off the box. "I peeked in the boxes. They're gorgeous and smell absolutely delicious."

Fiona had taken extra care in choosing the flowers for the house. "Since a lot of the guests will be wandering inside Hart House, we thought it would be a nice touch to add extra floral arrangements inside." She also had made it a point to order fresh magnolia blooms for a few key spots in honor of the bride.

Susan reached for a large apron from a nearby hook and tied it around her waist. "I'm so glad there's finally something I can help with. We're always entertaining for Carl's associates. Turns out I did a better job at flowers than the expensive florists. It's going to be fun doing this for my Kelly."

Katie glanced at Fiona and smiled. Despite some of the stories of Susan's flighty parenting skills, she was going to fit in just fine.

"It's all going to be so lovely." Fiona crossed the kitchen to fill the tea kettle. She had hoped to arrange the flowers herself, but Susan had been so excited to have found something she was good at that Fiona didn't mind stepping aside at all. "Especially now in the beginning of summer."

"As I said before, nothing like a little blizzard and power outage to bring a couple together," Lucy teased.

"Don't even go there." Fiona shot her friend and housekeeper a reproving glare.

"I haven't said a word." Lucy flashed a return toothy grin at her employer.

"So." Katie rubbed her hands together and pointed to the tub she'd set in the fridge. "That's the last of the lobster roll mix for the luncheon. How many more croissants have you got to bake?"

"This is the last batch. The rest are on the dining room table."

Eyes closed, Katie whiffed gently at the air and the delectable aroma of fresh baked goods. "If this is as big a hit as I think it's going to be, I may have to start ordering more croissants from Lily's for the season."

"Oh, that is a wonderful idea." Lucy nodded.

"It's going to be a fabulous hit." Susan looked over her shoulder, a selection of flowers already trimmed in the vase. "I had a taste. Couldn't find a better croissant in Paris and that lobster roll is to die for."

Katie grinned and gently bobbed her head at the

woman. "So kind of you to say."

"Kind my foot. It's the truth."

Fiona reached for a tea cup and caught a glimpse of Glenn and Kelly holding hands, making their way into the kitchen. There wasn't anything as sweet in this world as the adoration in a loving couple's eyes and the warmth of a newborn babe. Today she was delighted to share in one more wedding on the lake. "And here they come."

"How did the rehearsal go?" Poppy asked.

Still holding her fiancé's hand, and grinning like the Cheshire Cat, Kelly sank onto a stool beside Poppy. "Good thing Pastor Bob cues us to answer because I don't think I'm going to remember my own name."

Fiona set a hot cup of tea in front of Poppy and patted the back of Kelly's hand. "You'll do just fine. In all the weddings that have been held on this lake, we've never lost a bride."

"She's right, baby." Susan smiled at her daughter. "You'll be perfect."

"Thanks, Mama."

"That's certainly good to know." Glenn took his place behind his fiancée, his hands resting on her shoulders, gently kneading away the nervous tension. "Because truth be told, I may be a little nervous myself."

"Second thoughts?" Susan lifted one brow, her pleasant smile shifting to mama bear mode. Something Fiona was very pleased to see.

"Not even close." Glenn leaned over and kissed Kelly on the cheek then straightened. "I've never been more sure of anything in my entire life. I've just never been great in front of a crowd."

"But you perform in front of a crowd?" Poppy stared up at him.

Glenn shrugged. "I know, but that's different.

I'm hiding behind a massive piano."

"No problem," Lucy teased. "We'll have the pastor push the piano up to the altar."

"Don't you even think of it!" Fiona held back a laugh. She had watched so many people fall in love on Lawford mountain, from each of her daughters, to all nine of her granddaughters, and now the more extended family. It never ceased to amaze her how much love the human heart could hold. Eyes burning with love remained steady on Kelly. Briefly she lifted her face and her gaze met Glenn's. A silent word of thanks and appreciation was shared and Fiona knew deep in her soul that these two were going to make a long and happy life just like she and the General had. The thought made her smile.

"Okay, you two." Lucy waved a hand in the couple's direction. "Keep looking at each other like that and we're going to have to call Cole and his buddies in here to put out the fire."

"She's right." Callie reached around Lucy and swiped a cookie from the jar. "Save some of that for later."

The remainder of the rehearsal party filtered into the kitchen. Cindy and Kelly's maid of honor took seats at the small table. Iris shooed her kids, the flower girl and ring bearer, out the back door to play and had them take the dogs with them. Glenn's grandfather, who was going to walk the bride down the aisle, stood with his wife by the General, just taking in the commotion.

For Fiona, there was nothing like a gathering of family for a happy occasion. Setting her hand on her youngest granddaughter's shoulder, she lifted her chin in the direction of the tea she'd made. "You haven't touched your tea."

Poppy shook her head. "Not in the mood for tea."

"Drink it," Fiona encouraged. "It will make you feel better."

Her granddaughter's gaze met hers and she could tell Poppy was deciding what to say next. "You know?"

Fiona nodded. "Figured it out last week. I wasn't going to say anything until you did, but this will help."

"Thank you." The words came out soft and low and filled with love.

Standing at Fiona's other side; Katie slapped her hand against her heart. "Another year of great blessings."

It shouldn't surprise Fiona that Katie also knew Poppy's little secret.

"Three new additions to the Hart clan," Katie added a little louder.

"Three?" several nearby voices echoed.

Fiona glanced at her granddaughter and waited for Poppy to nod or nix making the announcement for all to hear.

"Yes," Fiona explained on her granddaughter's nod. "Our Cindy is married to Alan, which already made Alan family. Glenn is Alan's brother, which makes him family as well now. So that's the first one. Now Glenn is marrying Kelly, which makes her—"

"Family," the room echoed, including Glenn and Kelly.

"Which makes two. And of course," she waved a hand at Poppy, "a new baby to come makes three."

Squeals could be heard across the room. Chairs slid across the tile floor and Poppy was inundated with hugs and well wishes.

Clearing his throat, the General raised his glass in the air. "Congratulations and good cheer are in order for all the new family members."

Applause and whistles erupted, and Glenn recaptured his fiancée's hand. "Should we tell them?"

"It's nothing." Kelly blushed and Glenn shrugged.

"Oh, no." Lucy reached for the oven door. "You can't tease us like that."

The oven door open, the smell of perfectly baked croissants filled the room.

Lifting her nose to the air, Kelly sniffed. "I can't think straight with the aroma of fresh baked croissants. With butter, no less."

"There'll be no getting out of it. What's the secret we're all dying to hear?" Katie asked.

"It's not exactly a secret." Glenn squeezed Kelly's hand. Again.

"It's silly really. At the rehearsal, Pastor Bob said my full name."

"And I thought it was a perfect fit for the newest bride in the Hart clan."

"And?" Lucy prompted.

Kelly blew out a sigh. "My middle name is Magnolia."

Fiona slapped her hands together. *Another flower.*

Their fingers laced, Glenn lifted their hands to his lips and kissed Kelly's knuckles. "I have a little surprise for you."

"I'm not sure I can take much more right now," Kelly teased.

"I think you'll like this one." He turned to Fiona and nodded.

All last night Fiona had wrapped and rewrapped the gift as Glenn had asked, wanting it to be exceptionally special. She'd carefully hidden it out of the way and had been waiting for the signal. Pulling it from behind the pantry door, she handed it to Glenn.

"It took a little bit of legwork and agreeing to a charity performance in the fall, but I wanted you to have this."

The pretty pink paper topped with ribbons and bows drew everyone's attention. Carefully, one ribbon at a time, Kelly untied the gift, then peeled the tape. Anticipation filled the room as she continued to peel the paper away from what was obviously now a shoebox.

Her gaze drifted up to meet his and the air in the room grew even thicker with anticipation.

Slowly, she lifted the top off the box and her eyes popped open. "Oh, my." From the box, she lifted one red kitten heeled Jimmy Choo that looked very much like the one that Wooster had snacked on.

"Do you like them?"

"Like?" She sprang from the seat and threw her arms around his neck. "I love them!"

"I feel like Cinderella with the glass slipper." She kicked her old shoes off and slipped into the new ones. "Do you think there's any reason I couldn't wear red shoes with my white dress?"

"None at all." He pulled her closer into his arms and leaned in for a soft kiss. "I love you, Kelly."

"I love you too."

The room had returned to the chaos of preparing for the pre-wedding luncheon. More guests arrived but Fiona's heart remained full. So much devotion and adoration in both of her new family member's eyes. Yep. There wasn't a stitch of doubt in Fiona's mind, that these two were meant to be forever happy together.

Thank you for joining us on a return trip to Hart Land with Kelly and Glenn. Stay tuned for a new family series set in Texas ranch country from Chris.

If you're looking for more books from Chris, you can find her Aloha, Farraday Country, Honeymoon, and Hart Land series on her website:

https://www.chriskeniston.com/books.html

MEET CHRIS

Author of over thirty contemporary novels, Chris Keniston lives in suburban North Texas with her husband, two human children, and two canine children. Though she loves her puppies equally, she admits being especially attached to her German Shepherd rescue. After all, even dogs deserve a happily ever after.

Follow Chris on her weekly blog at chriskeniston.com,
on facebook at ChrisKenistonAuthor or on twitter @ckenistonauthor

Never miss a New Release! Sign up for News from Chris: www.chriskeniston.com/newsletter.html

Questions? Comments?
I would love to hear from you! You can reach me at: chris@chriskeniston.com